A SHEIKH GOT ME

RACHEL

JUST BAE

ISBN: 9781925988390

CONTENTS

CHAPTER ONE

*R*achel Johnson had suddenly awakened. Her eyes didn't want to open and she was dead tired. She moved her hands around to get some sense of where she was, but all she felt was something hard pressing against her.

"Where the hell am I?" Rachel spoke but didn't hear anything. She tried pushing herself up, but found something was over her eyes; a blindfold. She took it off and squinted as the sunlight beamed in from the windows.

As her vision adjusted to the light, she realized she was lying on the floor of a lavish room.

It was painted burgundy and had gold trimmings. Rachel was stretched out over a Persian carpet with a coat of arms with a dagger in the middle with words written Arabic.

There was a kingsize bed with a canopy that stood

proudly behind and dressers on each side with mirrors atop. To her right, was a small desk with a laptop and door she assumed led to the bathroom. There was another door to her left and a door in front.

As her hazel eyes settled on the one in front, it immediately opened. Two women dressed in abayas entered. They were short and speaking to each other in a foreign language. They looked like housekeepers or maids.

"Quum," one of the women said in a heavy accent. As Rachel struggled, the woman pulled her up and started looking over her. She examined and pinched Rachel's stomach and then lifted her breasts. Then, she went on checking Rachel's teeth and lastly tugged at her jeans, cupping her hips, and buttocks.

Rachel wasn't sure what was going on but these women made her feel uncomfortable. She was a girl from Atlanta who was curvy in all the right places.

"What size do you wear?" The older of the two asked in English.

"Eight."

The woman nodded as the second woman began taking Rachel's measurements.

"You will do. But hopefully better than the rest," said one of the woman. When they were leaving, Rachel stopped them.

"Can you please tell me where am I?"

"You're in Omash." The woman answered quickly before leaving.

"Omash?" "But that's halfway across the world, how did I leave America, I don't even have a passport. Oh God! "

She clutched her sides and began crying thinking about the horror stories of women being kidnapped and sold in Asia.

The women looked at her pitifully and exited the room. Minutes later, a young man came by and brought dates and a glass of water.

The late afternoon had come and Rachel mentally devised a plan for her escape. She remembered from history class Omash was closer to Africa than America. The only way to leave was by gaining someone's trust or stealing someone's stash.

"Maybe whoever's in charge will make me their slave? Oh, Hell, no!"

She shook her head at the thought when the two women came back. Rachel put on a front, smiling.

The oldest entered first. "Habiba, are you feeling better this evening?"

"Yes, I am. Thanks for the lamb and rice. It was delicious. By the way, what are your names?"

"I'm Maha and this is Hibba and we will be your personal helpers during your stay here in Omash," said the eldest.

Rachel saw Maha and Hibba as the perfect decoy when the time arises to escape.

"Nice to meet you, I'm Rachel. Do you know how I was brought here?"

"My dear, we cannot answer your questions. I'm truly sorry." Hibba nodded.

"You'll be fine. Omash is a beautiful place. You will like it," said Maha patting Rachel on the shoulder. "Now, come with us."

The women ushered Rachel out down the corridor. As they walked, Rachel was mesmerized by her surroundings. It was a beautiful palace and whoever owned it must have been very rich. There were beautiful sands and water surrounding the palace with a bridge on one side and dome structures to the left. Below was a beach and Rachel noticed a boat that looked vaguely familiar but couldn't understand why. She could only remember studying for her final exam at her local library. After grabbing a latte from the library's Starbucks, she couldn't remember anything else.

As they walked further, Maha spoke on how the palace had been in the Al Said Hamaad family for years. Her and Hibba would occasionally point out the rooms as they passed by through the palace's doors. So far, Rachel counted twelve. As Rachel observed the mosaic tiles that made up the walkways, she smelled food coming from the kitchen.

"Where exactly are you taking me? I'm not your slave."

"To the kitchen where you will meet the head-mistress."

Rachel was worried. She knew nothing about Arab culture and only heard a few people in her neighborhood say "Salam Alaykum" in passing.

As they entered, there was an older woman sitting at the table with a cane. Rachel smiled as Hibba and Maha pushed her forward.

"Salam Alaykum, I'm Atiyah." The woman extended her hand and Rachel took it and bowed. The woman chuckled and then told the young girl to sit.

Maha put a plate of food in front of Rachel. Rachel's stomach could be heard growling. She had no clue what was it was except for the vegetables and peppers.

"Eat my young child. It's a baraka." As Rachel dug in, Atiya told her more about her family's dynasty.

"For centuries, the rulers of Omash have been chosen from our lineage. We are a monarchy. When the ruler becomes too old to rule, he chooses a successor. Our family council also chooses a successor and if an agreement cannot be reached whoever was chosen by the previous family automatically becomes the leader."

"Ok, but why are you telling me this? You

kidnapped me and I want to go home. I got family back in America, you know?"

"May Allah forgive me for speaking so harshly dear but no one will miss you."

"Old lady, please don't go there. I'm being nice."

"You were chosen because of your beauty, fertility, and smarts. We know you have three siblings, all of which you are always fighting. We know you are very close to your mother but have become estranged over the years. We also know you have been living with a roommate while away at school. We like that you take care of her cat, Louie."

"God damn! What else do you know about me?"

"Hmm, we know you had two boyfriends in your entire life, you're 22 years old and that twins run in your family." Atiya said all of this from memory.

"Do you know what bra size too?" Rachel said sarcastically.

"40 D."

Rachel almost choked on her food. "Why the hell are you people want me so bad?" she asked wiping her mouth.

"That's an easy one. We've been following you all semester. Let's say you were handpicked and we didn't want to just pick anyone off the street. We only pick women with special traits to carry on our family lineage."

"Why the hell didn't you go on Tinder? Matter of fact, do you know if I'm even a virgin?"

"Yeah, your doctor's records show that you've been there quite often for mammograms."

"Again, why am I here?"

"Ya Allah, that's a simple one, too. You are here to give me grandchildren." Atiya said smiling.

"Oh, hell no! I'm not the one, old lady! Matter of fact, I need to leave. Now! "

"My Goodness, no my child! You, Americans and your reality shows like the Kardashians have given you such polutted ideas about us, Arabs. You're here to become the bride of my son and give him heirs. You will become queen one day."

Rachel looked at the old woman. *This lady must have gone mad.*

"Here have some tea, habiba." the old woman offered."My son is the sultan of Omash and in order to continue our lineage, we need you to bear his children."

"Again, Tinder, Plenty of Fish and Match.com will be your best options. Not me. I'm just a black girl from around the way."

"There are thousands of Omashi women who would love to bear his young but he keeps refusing them. We've tried to catch his interest with hundreds of girls online but all in vain. It seems that he has a liking for black girls. He also likes those who are strong and independent." Atiya looked winking her eyes at Rachel.

"Hmm, they say the melanin will get em'." Rachel pouted and folded her arms. She didn't like feeling controlled and outmatched.

"Look, Rachel you are a beautiful girl. I'm sure by now you've done the math and seen what we have to offer. My son is very rich and if you are chosen, you will be well taken care of. All I want is beautiful healthy grandchildren. If chosen, you will wed shortly after and begin mating."

"Excuse me, but I'm not someone's egg donor. There's a thing called love, you know?" Rachel stood up angrily.

Maha and Hibba cringed looking at their head-mistress who only smiled.

"You have a fiery passion that will suit my son well in the bedroom and in this life."

Rachel sat back down and slouched in her chair.

"Don't do that. It's very unladylike." Atiya went to sip on her tea.

"So what happens if I am not chosen?"

"Then you will be dropped off back with your family and this will all just be a dream. No one would believe you if you told them anyway."

"I wouldn't count on it. Once my brother sees you, he'll be rushing to give me nieces and nephews."
"Omi! " a man said entering the room and embracing the old woman.

"Haithum!"

Rachel looked at the handsome man and couldn't help but keep staring. She had to admit that if his brother looked anything like him, he may be worth staying around a few days.

As the two embraced, Rachel ended the motherly display of affection with a *q*question."If your other son has no heirs, why can't Mr. Haithum take over the throne?"

"I'm too old to rule and have no desire in such matters. I'm a happily married businessman that enjoys traveling and doing it up, you know?"

This boy is something else.

Rachel slumped in her seat seeing that there was no immediate way out of this.

"Lucky for us, my son is away on business and will not return for two and a half weeks. This will give us plenty of time to get you prepared for your first meeting and acquainted with our culture."

"Why teach me? Who says I even agree? And he might not like me anyway."

Haithum turned to Rachel grinning. "Oh no, he will. I know my brother. He likes what I like."

"Think, Rachel, Think." Rachel thought as she bit her lip still pissed. She knew during the next two and a half weeks, she'd have to come up with a plan to get away.

"What's your son's name?"

"Naseem."

"That's a black boy's name!"

"You like it?"

"Hmm, it's okay. I know a few of them back home."

"Now that you're full, it's time for your lessons to begin. A good Omashi woman knows how to take care of her husband. You must attend to his every need. We will start in the kitchen."

Atiya took Rachel to the kitchen which resembled that back off a high-scale restaurant. Rachel knew how to cook burgers, wings, and quick stuff but wasn't ready to be wifing nobody. There were utensils and pots that appeared to match each dish; all looked like they cost a fortune.

"Must be nice to be a sultan?"

"The first thing I will teach you to prepare tea and coffee. Hot drinks are very important in our culture, so knowing how to make these are necessary. Now, to make the tea, you want to first bring the tea bags and water to a boil."

"That should be easy," Rachel said turning the burner on high and placing a pot of water down.

"As we are waiting on that, please prepare one tablespoon of ginger and three tablespoons of sugar.

My son has a bit of a sweet tooth, so I'd add four just in case. Rachel followed instructions.

"Now that the water's boiling, you want to slowly add a can of evaporated milk with the sugar and bring it to a boil again."

The old woman had Rachel smiling for some odd reason.

"And now you are done, pour this into the teapot and let's start the coffee."

"But what about the ginger?"

"I'll take care of it, habibtee. I know how he likes it."

After two hours of being in the kitchen, Rachel was exhausted. The sun was beginning to set and she wanted to go to sleep.

"Before I let you go, I'd like to introduce you to two others who will be with you everywhere you go."

Rachel rolled her eyes.

"This is Rafiq and Hamid. Think of them as your bouncers. Wherever you go, they go and if you need anything, all you have to do is ask."

"Okay, hello—" Rachel said nodding but was amazed at their physique. She remember hearing it was improper to shake hands with Arab men, so she held hers back.

Rafiq and Hamid were brothers and both were buff and good-looking. Rafiq had blue eyes and Hamid's were gray and looked as if they lived in the gym. Rachel perceived Rafiq was the more approachable of the two.

"Tomorrow, Rafiq and Hamid will take you out shopping for more suitable garments," Atiya said looking at Rachel's clothes in displeasure."If my son keeps you as I anticipate, you will need some real clothes to wear. Not these tight things."

"Lady, I'm from America. This is what we wear. Don't be trying to come at me. Ok?"

"Habibtee, you are in Omash now. You must look like a queen."

"If you say so."

"Your bodyguards have been instructed on where to take you. Don't disrespect our kindness by trying to escape, are we clear?"

"Yes, Atiyah," said Rachel like a chastised child.

"Call me Omi, dear. Now run along and get some rest."

Rafiq and Hamid escorted Rachel back to her quarters.

CHAPTER TWO

"We will be waiting outside when you awake, Miss Rachel," said Rafiq.

Rachel entered and laid down. Before she could count to one hundred, she had fallen asleep.

When she woke up, she went to shower. The clock on the wall read 10:45 pm."These people really go out shopping this late," sighed Rachel as she stepped into the bathroom which was bigger than her dorm room. She saw a sunken tub with massaging jets with eight gears and a button to adjust the heat.

To her left, was a sink with a gold faucet and above it were marble counters. The rugs on the floor had the same coat of arms as in the living room while shower curtains had the same. Her favorite bath soaps and salts were lined up on the shelves.

"They really have done their research. Haven't they?" Rachel said opening a bottle of Moonlight

Path. She took her clothes off and showered. After fifteen minutes she got out and realized she had no clean clothes. When she came out, her servant, Maha holding an outfit.

"My lady, we have fresh clothes for you."

Rachel stared at the closet full of garments in her room. "Wow! How did you get these clothes so quickly in my size?"

"Our seamstresses have been at work since I took your measurements earlier."

"Can you help me with this?" Rachel said after putting on a dress and trying to fix the matching hijab.

After helping her out, Rachel walked out and was immediately accompanied by Rafiq and Hamid. When she went got to the entrance, they told her the shops were all close for the night.

"Well, you could have said something." Rachel pouted as she went back to her room.

———

The next day Maha and Hibba woke Rachel up at 10 am. Donning the dress she wore last evening, they told her to put on a face veil.

"Oh, hell no! I'm not putting that on."

"My lady, our society is very conservative. Please don't give us trouble," said Maha.

Dressed in a black face veil, Rachel left out with Rafiq and Hamid.

The market place was unlike anything Rachel had ever seen before. There were teas, incenses, spices, rugs, silks, and pottery spread on the grounds. Children ran and played while men walked through with camels and women were laughing at a fountain as they ate sweets. Rachel also saw a few children playing with dogs that Hibba called Salukis.

The place was so beautiful and peaceful.

They entered deeper inside; Rachel was surrounded by her bodyguards. Maha led them to a boutique called Aya.

"We've been expecting you. Salam alaykum."

"Wa alaykum as-Salam," said Rachel.

Maha explained before coming that Rachel should pick out long dresses and robes in dark colors. Unlike the American dresses, these garbas had patterns where a woman's cleavage and skin would normally show. Rachel was in awe of how much work went into tailoring them.

"It would be nice to have some scarfs with these also," said Rachel grabbing a few items.

The shopowner, Maha and Hibba helped Rachel pick out a few pairs of sandals to go with each overgarment.

After an hour, the group was ready to go back to the palace. The sun's heat was overwhelming. When they arrived, Maha escorted her to the kitchen to Atiya. The old woman had lunch already prepared. After a small chat, Atiya gave Rachel more lessons on making traditional Arabic dishes until the late afternoon.

CHAPTER THREE

*M*ost of Rachel 's time ten days later were spent with Atiya learning how to cook, manners and small customs. Although the palace had a few chefs, Naseem's mother thought it was important Rachel learn from her. She knew exactly how to make her son's favorite dishes.

Although this kept Rachel busy, she felt lonely and homesick. Maha would come by and keep her company and for that Rachel was grateful but most of the time, Maha didn't understand what Rachel was talking about.

"You should be happy." Maha said one afternoon. "You have lasted longer than most."

"That is only because your master hasn't returned yet and dismissed me," whispered Rachel as the two continued cutting vegetables.

"I'm very excited about your progress, Rachel,"

said Atiya from the other side of the kitchen. Maha was signaled to leave the room.

Although Atiya appeared strict, Rachel couldn't help but like the woman. Earning her favor was beginning to become obtainable.

"Thank you, Omi. You're a good teacher."

Although she'd never admit it, Rachel loved the shoutouts from Atiya. It reminded her of her mother when they were still getting along.

"Maha and Hibba have told me how you've been moping around."

Rachel looked away.

"Because you've been good so far, I decided to buy you a present."

Unless it's a one-way ticket back to America, I'd cheer up.

"It's waiting for you in your room. Enjoy the weekend off. I'll be out of town until Monday. Just in time, when you will meet you new instructor who will teach you the art of seduction."

Rachel put her hand on her mouth as the old woman left the kitchen accompanied by her bodyguards. She couldn't help but wonder what was left in her bedroom.

When she opened the door, she gasped at what was lying on her bed; boxes of her things from her old apartment. Her books of poetry, a bracelet - her brother gave her for her birthday, the last photo she had taken with her family, her favorite Spelman hoodie, clothes, underwear and a few pairs of shoes.

Rachel was ecstatic as she started unpacking and putting them on display around her room. A moment of happiness touched her until she held the portrait of her family. She hoped they were looking for her.

At that moment, the laptop clicked on the desk. Rachel went to see if it was connected online.

Why hadn't I thought of this sooner? I can send my mom an email, so they can get me the hell out of here!

As Rachel hit the power button, she crossed her fingers and stared at the screen.

"Come on, come on, please don't ask for a password."

"Shit! " The password screen came up and Rachel sat there pondering her next move.

Rachel opened her door. Thank God, her bodyguards were nowhere to be found. She crept down the hall toward the library, checking each corridor as she crossed. She heard the maids in the kitchen talking. As she turned down the last corridor, she sighed; glad she had made it.

"Going somewhere?" a deep voice startled her.

"No, I'm just—" Rachel gasped turning around. "Are you trying to give me a heart attack, Rafiq?"

Rafiq laughed taking a bite of his apple."Where were you trying to go, my lady?"

"To the library—" Rachel began and came up short.

"Research?"

"Research—Right!

"Seriously, How can I help?"

Rachel wondered if she should tell him she was trying to use the computer or just lie. The girl really hated lying.

She decided to go with a partial truth instead."I was trying to use a computer. I wanted to check my grades for last semester which should be in by now as well as some other stuff—"

Rafiq raised his eyebrow not convinced. He then chuckled

"What's so funny?"

"You're up to something. The master would be a fool to underestimate you. Come with me. There's a laptop in your room."

When they got back, Rafiq signed her in and stood by watching.

Keeping her word, Rachel checked her school's website. While waiting on the page to load, she checked her email and Twitter page.

Her emails weren't important so she deleted most. There were a few messages on Twitter from her friends asking if she wanted to get together for drinks this weekend to going to the movies which she saw as weird. Rachel had been gone for nearly two weeks and yet no one called the cops to report her missing.

"Rafiq, can I ask you something?"

"Yes, my lady."

"Did you guys by any chance leave a note saying I would be gone for a while?"

"No ma'am. Not that I know of."

Rachel was hurt, why wasn't anyone looking for her? She knew at times she was a loner but never thought at least one person would notice her missing. And then she remembered at the beginning of the semester, she had been bragging about taking a trip overseas. Her friends probably assumed that she had gone away right after exams.

Clicking from her Twitter page to her school website, Rachel saw she finished the semester with a 3.8 GPA.

It was the only thing that made her smile.

"Congratulations."

"Thanks, but it's not going to do me good here."

"Allahu A'lam."

"What does that mean?"

"God knows best."

Rafiq logged off and Rachel grabbed a romance novel from her box called She Got Me: The Perfect Ending. Rafiq took it as a cue to leave.

After five chapters of the hot steamy story, Rachel put the book down and fell asleep.

CHAPTER FOUR

*M*onday morning, Maha escorted Rachel to another area of the palace where she'd never been. Walking through two huge mahogany doors, Rachel looked around as they stepped inside a ballroom. Polished oak covered its length and the artwork of the Hamaad family were on full display on both sides. As Rachel looked above, sunlight penetrated landing perfectly and making the floor shine even brighter. Maha left and brought a woman back dressed in dance attire.

"Rachel , this is Dania, she will be your instructor."

"Hello."

"Marhaban."

Maha then left the room.

"I will be teaching you Raqs Sharqi. The westerners call it belly dancing."

"I already know how to dance, ma'am. Thanks."

"Raqs Sharqi is not what you westerners are doing. I've watched a lot of your Beyonce and Rihanna videos. This is a bit more seductive, my lady. Dancing is an art, you must enter, arouse your audience, but still be able to keep your secrets," said Dania as she began dancing slowly. Rachel watched on as her moves were captivating.

"People spend years trying to master this art. It's very difficult for non-Arabs."

"I'm willing to learn something new." Rachel said getting into position.

Then let's start."

"Iftaahul-Mooseeca, Hamid."

After another four-hour practice with Dania, Rachel was worn out. She has been practicing daily. Her hips were always sore and the only good thing about learning was it was a great workout.

After taking a shower, Rachel went to the kitchen to make something to eat. She had on her Spelman hoodie and denim shorts which was showing her ass cheeks. As she stirred the pot, she mulled over what to do. The sultan was returning in less than a week and Rachel still had no clue how to escape.

As she chopped up some beef cubes, she sang her

favorite song, Crazy in Love which took her mind off the pains in her abs.

Meanwhile, outside of the palace, a Black Mercedes pulled up and a tall well-dressed man stepped out.

"Sayyid Naseem, we weren't expecting you." A servant said as he rushed to greet him.

"I missed home, Bashir." Naseem said looking tired. He saw the startled look in Bashir's eyes and others as they hustled to take his things.

"Ajeeb! " Naseem thought finding everyone looking nervous.

"Please send Rafiq to my quarters right away." Naseem said heading to the kitchen to grab something to eat.

The servants covered their mouths as they watched Naseem walk towards the kitchen. He knew something was off by the scent. Once he got near the kitchen door, he saw Rafiq standing on guard.

"Rafiq, my friend. Salam alaykum." Naseem embraced.

"Sayyudna. Marhaban." Rafiq said as his eyebrows scrunched.

"Is anyone around here going to tell me what's going on?"

After staring at Rafiq, Naseem went inside. A heavenly aroma drew him in but a lighter scent clouded it.

"Who's cooking?" Naseem thought.

Once he stepped further inside, he saw Rachel ass cheeks in perfect postion as she hovered over the stove. She was unaware of Naseem's presence still singing and slowly stirring the contents inside the pot. He was amazed by her body. Rachel was barefoot and Naseem stood in amazement.

"Now this is a welcome home I can get used to." Naseem thought as he took off his jacket. He licked his lips gazing at this black woman up and down. She was his type for sure. Naseem envisioned her soft hands massaging his sore muscles after stripping him.

What was this woman doing here? Was she the new maid?

"Hello." Naseem cleared his throat causing Rachel to jump. She dropped the ladle in the pot.

"Darn it, Rachel. Stop jumping every time a man says something to you."

"Hi." Rachel said as she turned and then gaped. In front of her, was the most handsome man she had ever seen.

Damn, he looks like he just stepped off the runway, in that tailored black suit. Look at those brown eyes and black hair that's peaking out from under his scarf.

"This man's sexy as shit," Rachel kept pondering. She bet he had women gushing over him. Naseem was an orgasm just waiting to happen and Rachel's nipples hardened as these delicious thoughts overcame her.

"Stop it! " she thought blushing and turning away.

"And who are you?"

"I'm Rachel." Rachel tried once again to fetch the ladle out the pot.

"You have our kitchen smelling like heaven, Miss Rachel." Naseem said coming closer, taking a whiff of the food and her scent.

Rachel could have came right there. "He smells so divine," she thought as he moved in closer. Rachel had to force herself not to do anything stupid.

"Here, let me help you with that." Naseem reached down close to her ass. Before Rachel could move away, he'd opened the drawer and pulled out a longer ladle; using it to pull the other one from the pot.

"See all better."

Meanwhile, Naseem thought his brother brought her here as the new maid. *"I'll have to thank him when I am finished."*

"Rachel , what brings you here, if I may ask?"

"Well, I—" she stuttered.

"You—I—" Naseem said putting his warm hands on her shoulders and lightly caressed them.

"I—I" Rachel stuttered, completely enraptured by his spell. She bit her lips as she stared into his eyes. Before she could even blink, she was in Naseem's arms and his lips were descending on hers. The ladle once again was forgotten and had fallen back into the pot.

"I don't even know who he is? Do I even care?"

Somehow Naseem's touch felt so right. Instead of

scaring Rachel like a man's touch usually did, it felt overwhelming and protecting. The first touch of their lips sent a line of fire coursing through them. Rachel moaned and moved in closer, as Naseem gripped her ass. Feeling bold, she waggled her tongue in between his lips while dueling with his.

"I just have to have a taste of this man," she thought as she felt Naseem's hard dick pressing against her and it was hard as fuck. That feeling thrilled but terrified her at the same time. Rachel did not want to stop, but refused to get carried away with this stranger. She pulled back and Naseem let her go.

Stupid, stupid girl. What are you doing? Focus! How are you going to get out of here now?

Awkwardly, she coughed and tucked her hair nervously behind her ear as she licked her reddened lips.

"I must have lost the ladle again," she giggled.

Ugh, what's wrong with me! One kiss by this Arab and I'm giggling like a school girl.

Naseem reached around her and fetched the ladle out. His thoughts were overwhelming. Although she responded to his call, it was clear Rachel was not experienced.

"Rachel, why are you here again?" Naseem asked running a hand through his hair.

"Well, I am—" Rachel began.

"She's our new maid." Atiya said entering the room, freshly arrived from her trip.

"She's a harem girl." His brother Haithum said at the same time holding his mother's bags.

Naseem was puzzled and Haithum countered. "She's a harem girl that works as a maid."

His brother's words effectively doused the tension between Naseem and Rachel and sparked a different kind of fire.

"Now you listen here, Mr. Haithum," Rachel said angrily stepping around Naseem. "I'm no damn prostitute. It's bad enough I'm being held against my will here."

"Rachel! " Atiya cut her off, "What in the world are you wearing, my child?"

Rachel looked down at her booty shorts and raised her hands. She hated being chastised and knew she was wrong.

"Sorry, Ms. Atiya, I thought there were no men around. I was making myself dinner when Mr—came in." Rachel stopped and looked at Naseem.

"Please go and change. Come back when you are properly dressed."

"I am."

"Go, my child now."

"Ok." Rachel pouted leaving quickly with Rafiq.

When Rachel left, Naseem turned toward his brother and mother. He put two and two together guessing

Rachel wasn't a maid or harem but another ploy from his family to get him married.

My mother must be pretty desperate if she brought this one all the way from America.

"More of your tricks to see me married off?" said Naseem. His mother looked away innocently.

"You must admit brother, she's a very attractive." Haithum kept grinning. "Attractive, hot, and—"

"Boys stop this talk now!"

"Ok, Omi."

"Naseem, did you see the way she stood up to your brother. This woman will never bore you."

"What makes her so different from the others?"

Naseem didn't like being boxed in. Even if she was beautiful, he wanted to make his own choices.

"You can't say you're not the least bit fascinated by her—?" said Haithum.

"I said stop it!" Atiya yelled in Arabic.

"How? I only spent a few seconds with her."

"Fine then, I'll make her one of my harem girls. A maiden of her beauty will suit me well."

"Ya Ghabee, didn't I say stop it. One more time and I'll—"

"Haithum, my brother, you don't have a harem and you are madly in love with your wife."

"I could start with that one."

Atiya picked up a broom and started hitting Haithum with it.

"Ok, Omi. I'll stop."

"Let me have dinner with her and decide. If she's unworthy, she'll go back home untouched. Understood?"

"Ok, brother." Haithum smiled as his brother played right into his hands.

Haithum knew Rachel had left a lasting impression on his brother and so did Atiya.

"No one is to tell her who I am. Not yet. Make sure the servants know this as well," commanded Naseem.

Atiya and Haithum nodded as Naseem left the kitchen.

CHAPTER FIVE

*T*en minutes later, Rachel arrived back downstairs. dressed in a light-brown blouse tucked in with tan blazers. Back in her room, she had given herself a pep talk; admitting there was sexual chemistry between her and Naseem, but she had to focus on the task at hand.

When she entered the kitchen, she was surprised to see Naseem sitting alone at the table. Naseem looked up and asked,"Is there something wrong, my lady?"

"No, it's just...I wanted to thank your mother for being so patient with me. Ah well!"

"Would you like some soup?" Rachel said gesturing at the pot on the stove.

"Yes. Thanks."

Rachel made two bowls and sat two seats down.

She was grateful they weren't completely alone. Maha and Hamid were standing in the far corner.

"Why are you sitting so far away, habibtee? I won't bite."

But that's all Rachel could think about was Naseem biting her nipples, neck, and all the way down to her clit.

"I thought it wouldn't be right. I got chastised about what I wear around here, so who knows?"

"Don't worry. Come. There's no one else joining us."

"If you say so."

There was silence for a few minutes while they ate, but the sexual tension still exist. Their legs were so close that Rachel could feel the heat radiating off of Naseem's thigh through her pants. She licked her lips thinking of all the delicious sensations Naseem had stirred in her earlier. Trying to suppress the feeling, Rachel started up a small conversation.

"So Mr. Naseem, are you the other brother of the sultan?"

"Yes, I am."

"Hmm, okay."

"Do you have brothers, Rachel?"

"Yeah, I have three, but we're not very close. We all started living our separate lives after high school."

"That's too bad. Will you try to be closer to them when you go back?"

"Of course, family is everything. I want a big one day." Rachel paused eating and then asked,"Are you in business like your brothers?"

"Yes, I own a few. In fact, while I'm in town, I'll take you to a few."

"I'd love that. Anything to get away from here. A sister needs some fresh air, you know?" "By the way, will you be in town for a while?"

"Not sure. I may have a few deals coming up that will take me away again."

"So tell me more about Miss Rachel?" Naseem started smiling."I want to know all about my brother's future wife."

"Oh, you got things twisted, Mr. Naseem. I don't intend on marrying." As Rachel spoke, Rafiq could be heard clearing his throat.

"Why not? He's a rich man and can give you everything you could ever dream of."

"With all due respect, Mr. Naseem, money isn't everything. Marriage is a serious commitment and the man I marry must have--let's just say certain qualities."

"Really? What qualities?" Naseem was amused.

"Well for starters, he must be loyal. I will not share my husband with another woman."

"It's common practice for a sultan to have more

than one woman. What makes you think you will be different?"

"Let's rewind that back. I'm not marrying the Sultan. Now to answer your question, I'm sure I can keep my husband's sex drive in check. He won't need another chick, believe me!"

"What if he wants more chicks to bear more children?"

"I will bear all of his and keep delivering until he says enough."

Rachel dared Naseem to continue. She refused to let him get the best of her as he was beginning to get under her skin in more ways than one.

"Very well. So what other qualities should your husband have?"

"He must be honest, kind, cute and have some swag."

"Are you talking about a husband or a pet?" Naseem said joking.

"Very funny, Mr. Ay-Raab."

"Low blow—Go on."

"Well, I'd like it if my husband was sexy and of course, not full of himself."

"That's me," thought Naseem.

"This girl is definitely a hopeless romantic. Either that or the juicy romance novels in her boxes were getting to her," thought Naseem.

"And most importantly, I would like it if—" Rachel continued but was cut off.

"If—Rachel?"

"He was my protector," finished Rachel with a look of vulnerability. Before Naseem could say something, Rachel came to her senses.

"You have a long list of what you want."

Rachel then laughed.

"What's so funny?"

"Nothing, it's just--this sounds like a date."

"Somehow, I get the impression it would be hard to get you on one."

"Depends?"

"Ok, but are you hard to get?

"I can be—picky. I rarely went out back home."

Focus on the plan, Rachel. Don't let this Arab boy get you.

"What about you?" Rachel continued."I couldn't help but notice that you're easy on the eyes. A prince like you must have women knocking down your door and falling at your feet. You see what happened to me earlier."

"I do, but just like in business, I make wise decisions," answered Naseem as he took a sip of water.

"So, in other words, you're chosey?"

"I am. But I think it has worked to my benefit so far."

"I heard that." Rachel began sipping as well.

"So tell me more about your life back in the states, what did you do?"

"Well, I just finished my Bachelor's at Spelman in Biohemistry. I worked my way through college as a cashier at Pizza Hut and Starbucks. Both jobs were on campus. I had a roommate named Jessica and we lived with her cat, Louie."

"Which university? And what degree?"

"Spelman University and Biochemisty. Were you not paying attention?"

"Oh! I'm sorry, my lady. Those words I never heard of."

It was very clear Rachel had a lot of different personalities.

"So, back to your question. I want to research the latest pharmaceuticals, specifically those that help with pain relief and aid cell regeneration."

"Hmm, that's sounds complicated. What made you choose this field?"

"Well, my father. He started my interest in science. We were very close to him when I was younger and that was his passion. He passed away before I turned thirteen. It would be nice to do something that can help people with degenerative diseases in his honor."

"I'm sorry to hear about your father's passing."

"Yeah, it sucks. He was a good man."

"Please, enjoy your meal. Don't let me disturb you any longer," Naseem said getting up abruptly.

"Hamid!"

"Nam, Sayyidi."

"Have Rafiq meet me in my brother's office."

"Nam, Sayyidi." Hamid said as he stepped out.

"Excuse me, my lady. See you again soon."

"No problem."

Rachel felt a little disappointed by Naseem leaving all the sudden. She wondered if she had said something wrong.

"Maha, please come sit with me." Rachel requested as Hamid entered back inside.

"But my lady, it is not proper for servants to sit at the table with honored guests."

"I won't tell if you won't." "And you won't tell either Rafiq, will you?"

"No, Sayyida."

"Good and I'll be sure to leave you a bowl of my precious stew."

Rachel winked causing him to blush.

Meanwhile in Naseem's office...

"You can't tell me she hasn't gotten under your skin."Haithum sat in front of his brother's desk. Rafiq came and stood near the door.

"What makes you think she has?" said Naseem facing a window, overlooking the beach. The moonlight shining over the breaking waters lit his brooding face.

"Look at you over there." "Tell me what bothers you the most, brother. The fact that you will have to wait for Mrs. Right or the fact that you have met your match?"

"What makes you think I have met my match?"

"This one won't be some easy girl. Spend time with her and you'll see. We picked her for a reason."

"And what reason was that?

"She's a good one."

"Ajaal. I think you're right. She's gotten under my skin already," said Naseem blushing.

"I assume I can tell the servants she'll be staying for a while?"

Naseem was once again looked out the window, but this time he smiled as he saw Rachel walking. She was laughing at something Hibba was saying. Hamid was trailing behind.

"Haithum, what do you Omi think about this black woman?"

"She thinks she'll suit you well, sultan."

"Tayyib," said Naseem stroking his goatee. "And how about your brother Hamid? Would he agree?"

Rafiq nodded.

Naseem turned to his brother and said,"Tell the servants she will be staying indefinitely. Inform Umi, she can begin the wedding preparations quietly at once."

With that said, Naseem walked out of the room.

"Where are you going, brother?"

"I'm going to prepare myself for bed."

———————

Rachel walked back to the front of the palace followed by Hibba, Maha, and Hamid after a long morning walk. She was feeling a bit better after meeting Naseem yesterday. Something about him just made her feel good.

"Nothing like meeting a handsome man to lift a girl's spirits," Rachel daydreamed. Then, she was startled when she abruptly ran into a pillar. She put her arms out to prevent her fall but to no avail. A man's hands braced her and pulled her up.

"I'm sorry, Mr. Naseem," said Rachel looking up into his brown eyes. "I didn't see you coming."

"No worries." Naseem held her close. "Where are you off to this morning?"

"Your mother has informed me I'll be staying for a while longer until the master returns. There's been a delay of some sort which really sucks."

"I'm sorry for that."

"Well, she did give me a platinum card to go shopping for whatever I want. Will you come with me?"

"I don't know. Women shopping here is a private affair."

"I'm not buying that BS. I'm sure with all the women you've dated, you have a lot of experience."

Hibba, Maha and Rafiq laughed.

Rachel leaned in closer and whispered,"No offense, but Maha and Hibba are too old to tell me what's stylish. I wouldn't want to offend the sultan with my new attire." Rachel looked at Naseem ogling him.

"Well, since you put it that way, how can I say no?

"Good." Rachel had him right into her hands.

"Rafiq, have Bashir bring the other car around." Naseem ordered as he escorted Rachel out the gates.

When Rachel saw two cars out front, she couldn't hide her distaste.

"Does an American woman not like Mercedes?" Naseem asked.

"I always said if I ever had loads of money, I'd buy myself a Rapide S Aston Martin.""If you have the money, why not treat yourself?"

"Expensive cars for college students." Naseem replied catching Rachel offguard.

"Damn, a black girl can dream!" Rachel said as she entered into the GL63 AMG Mercedes SUV with Maha and Hibba.

————————

The women rode together while the men followed closely behind. When they arrived at the marketplace, the town appeared to stop for Naseem. Everyone came up and grasped his hands, talking to him in Omashi. When Rachel asked Maha what they were saying, she was told they were thanking him and his family for their generosity.

Naseem smiled at the people and Rachel looked on in awe.

"I see why these people like him," Rachel thought, as she continued walking with the entourage.

Instead of going to the first clothing shop, Naseem took Rachel to a boutique where the young women of Omash frequented. She instantly fell in love with the selection. The attire was modest but trendier. In addition to the embroidery, the garbs had different jewels, flowers, beads and chains on them. They also showed more of Rachel's curves and she liked that. Rachel tried on many dresses asking Naseem for his consent. Some he liked while others he nixed before she even tried them on.

Maha took Rachel over to the accessories area with some instructions from Atiyah. Rachel was in 7th heaven seeing the expensive lingerie. The feeling of having on lace panties under her clothes and no one knowing made her feel womanly. With the help of Maha and Hibba secretly, Rachel picked out many without Naseem seeing.

"Why not have a little fun while I'm here," mused Rachel as she picked out panties in her favorite colors. After getting some shoes, the group decided to end their shopping trip as it was nearing sunset.

Instead of going back to the palace, Naseem instructed his men to drive to one of his offices in town. Rachel was amazed at the sights of Omash along the way.

On the outskirts, there were small villas with children playing, women hanging clothes and fountains on every street. The closer they got to the inner town, the more buildings and crowded it became.

The city was an architectural dream and reminded Rachel of Dubai. It seemed like every architect tried to outdue the next with a better design. There were glass buildings casting shadows on the blue-green waters that were now almost black due to nightfall.

The group arrived outside a high-rise office building shaped like a tidal wave. Naseem got out first followed by Rafiq and Hamid.

"I'll only be a minute." He said as he passed by Rachel 's window.

"Ok."

After ten, Rachel decided to go inside herself.

"Sayyida Rachel! Sayyida Rachel! The master would not like it if you took off alone," said Hibba racing after her.

After going inside, Rachel reached the front desk displaying the Hamaad logo in gold letters in the background.

"I don't think Naseem will mind me coming up."

"My lady, it is haram to enter upon him unan-nounced."

"Don't worry, I got this."

At the elevators, she asked Hibba what floor was his office. Hibba told her she never been inside this building. "Ok, let's guess. There are 40 floors in this building, so I'm going to pick floor twenty-two."

When they reached the 22nd floor, there were chemistry labs. Rachel saw the equipment and smiled in awe; reminiscing about her lab days back in Spelman. She grabbed a coat and goggles and entered inside. Hibba tried stopping her but it was no use.

"Do you know what you are doing, my lady?"

"Oh, yes I do. I just graduated with a biochemistry degree."

Hibba put her hand over her nose from the smell and told Rachel to hurry and she would wait be outside.

Meanwhile, Naseem, Rafiq and Hamid had reached his office on the 41st floor. Naseem went inside and once he got the folder he came for, they got back on the elevator.

"So what do you think of your future wife, Sayyidana?" asked Rafiq.

"She's beautiful, but I can tell she will be a handful."

"You don't know half of it, Sayyidina," Rafiq said showing Naseem and Hamid the latest surveillance footage of the building on his smartphone. Hibba and Rachel got off on the 22nd floor.

"Looks like they got off on ithnaan wa ishreen," Hamid said hitting the elevator button.

"Such are women, they will always drive us crazy."

The men laughed as they went down.

CHAPTER SIX

Meanwhile on the 22nd floor.

"*O*h, my God! this lab got a GC-MS. Oh! and a MALDI," said Rachel touching the machines. She went around the room checking out everything until she saw a photo on a lab technician's desk. There was a man standing next to Naseem and it had a handwritten message. Rachel could not make it out but Naseem's name was signed in English.

"I knew it! I don't know who he thinks he's playing. I'll get him before he gets me. He's the prince."

Outside, Naseem was flanked by Rafiq and Hamid now arriving on the 22nd floor.

"Sayyidina, I tried to stop her—" Maha began but was stopped by Naseem's hand.

"Say nothing else. Return to the car at once with Rafiq and Hamid. Yallah!"

Once they boarded, Naseem entered the lab to see what his future bride was up to. He watched her gently touch the instruments for a minute before interrupting.

"Were you always a little curious chemist at heart or do you take me lightly?"

"Chemistry has always ran through my veins," Rachel answered stroking the tops of the test tubes. She smiled as she turned towards him.

"Why chemistry? Why not business or something more interesting?" Naseem teased as he stepped closer.

"Chemistry has always sparked me. It's life."

"It's the air you breathe and the water you drink. It explains nearly everything about you."

So, chemistry makes the world go round?"

Rachel stepped closer. "Especially the chemistry between humans."

"How so?" He asked as she invaded his space.

"Chemistry is electricity." Rachel said trailing her finger up his arm.

"Hmm… I see."

"That tingling sensation; the warmth you feel as I come on to you—" Rachel breathed deeply as she placed her hand on his chest,"That's what you call chemistry. Your body's energy is responding while deciding what it wants."

Rachel tried her best to put up a good front. When she tried to pull away, Naseem stopped her.

"So this feeling right here—" Naseem gently started kissing her on the neck. "Is this chemistry?" He continued going up and down. It made Rachel moan.

Naseem moved his hands down to her ass. They didn't stay there for long. Soon, he gripped her cheeks, he moved his hands higher to her hardened breasts. Before it was over, Rachel was on a lab bench with Naseem fondling her most tender spots.

"Naseem, boy. Stop!" Rachel moaned softly as Naseem licked her nipples. Hearing his name moaned from her lips was the sweetest delicacy.

I have to get control of myself.

Rachel could barely think straight with all of the pleasure Naseem was stirring inside her. Her pussy was so wet and she never let a man invade her like this.

Oh my God! This boy. He got me—? I have to stop him before it goes there.

"Naseem...Naseem...(Rachel moans)...Naseem, stop!"

When Naseem looked, he realized Rachel was somewhat serious.

"Why not give him some now?" said a little voice in Rachel's head.

She got down off the lab bench. "Boy, you're playing with fire. You know? I'm not yours," said Rachel as she fixed her clothes.

"I don't understand what you mean?"

"If I am your brother's, the sultan wouldn't like it if someone else touched something that's his."

Pulling Rachel toward him, Naseem said,"Well maybe, I'll have you and he won't."

"Good luck with that, buddy. I'm not a hoe."

Naseem then told her to go down and he'll be right there. Rachel was kind of glad as she needed time to get herself together and cool off before she saw the others.

CHAPTER SEVEN

*T*he next day, Rachel came downstairs for breakfast with a hop in her step, smiling. Naseem was already downstairs eating breakfast.

"Your maid, Hibba told me the sultan will be returning tomorrow and that the house will be having a dinner party," said Rachel as she made a plate. "Do you think your brother would allow me to work in his lab where we were the other day?"

"As the sultan's wife, you'll have other duties to attend to. Rather, it's not proper for her to work."

"Well, I now have a degree and maybe it may be frowned upon here, I'm from America and I need my space. Geesh! it's no longer the dark ages."

"I don't think my brother will agree. Besides, there will be plenty of things here to keep you busy."

"Like what exactly? I'm not getting you." Rachel folded her arms.

"That's more of my mother's expertise. I'm sure she'll tell you what your duties will be as the sultan's wife, that is if you agree."

"I'm sure I can convince your brother so it will make us one big happy family. By the way, don't try to lock down us, black people. You won't like us when we're angry." Rachel rose from the table with her plate and cup.

"I'm sure you're right," Naseem said as he watched Rachel sway her hips seductively as she walked away.

"Ya, Rabbee!"

"What was that?"

"Nothing, my lady. Just a prayer."

"Make one for me as well."

"This is the most delicious torture." Naseem thought as he watched Rachel from across the room. His mother hosted a party for the so-called Sultan's return. Naseem had asked his little brother to act in his place for the time being. He stood on the far side of the ballroom and watched as his youngest brother Fadi talking with Rachel. Rachel, in the meantime, was ravishing in her dark silk green dress. Its length kept her covered but clung to her like a second layer of skin. Her hair was wrapped in a bun that her hijab couldn't hide. She had five gold bangles on her arms and a gold necklace that fell in between her cleavage.

Naseem couldn't keep his eyes off her and neither could his brother, Fadi.

"Why ask for the charade if you cannot handle it, brother?" Haithum said coming to Naseem's left intruding on his brother's space.

"Wallahi, I don't know what you're doing. Tell her the truth, bro and make her yours."

"It's not that simple."

"Or is it?"

Naseem looked at him and took a sip of his drink as they watched everyone having a good time.

Rachel looked enraptured in Fadi's conversation. Inside, she felt as if her head would explode. She was turned on by Naseem and as charming as Fadi was, she would much rather be with his brother. Still, she was upset about what he said about working in the lab.

Rachel wondered how much longer would Naseem keep pretending. He really didn't have to. As far as the marriage was concerned, she hadn't even figured that part out yet. She liked him but being married was a fantasy she hadn't considered at the age of twenty-two.

"I'm so confused."

Out of the corner of Rachel's eye, she saw Naseem looking at her. She reached over and grasped Fadi arm laughing at something he said. She saw

Naseem clench his glass as if he was going to break it and it made her chuckle. Rachel enjoyed teasing him as Fadi continued talking. He thought foolishly that may be able to compete with his brother for Rachel. As soon as he saw the icy daggers Naseem was shooting him from across the room, he quelled the notion out of fear.

Rachel excused herself to check on the refreshments and went to the kitchen. Afterward, she went outside to the patio to stare at the moonlight. This had become one of her favorite distractions. Rachel loved the beauty of Omash at night.

The time was ticking away as Rachel sat with her feet in the sand. She closed her eyes and faced the sky taking in its aroma.

"Enjoying yourself?" Naseem approached.

"Very much so." Rachel shivered and Naseem took off his jacket and put it on her shoulders.

"I think I'll say yes to your brother's proposal."

"Really?"

"Even though, I don't like the fact I was kidnapped here, the sultan appears to be a good guy. He's agreed to all of my demands so far."

"What are these demands you're referring to?"

"Well, for starters. Your brother has agreed to allow me to work in the lab at his office."

"Does he know about—?" said Naseem chuckling.

"No."

"Good."

"However, it took little convincing, let's just say." Rachel said smiling. "I think there was love at first sight."

"Ok, so you—?"

"Do you want to see how I convinced him?" She said, ignoring Naseem and standing up pulling him. Rachel began singing a Rihanna song and they began dancing. Rachel put her arms around him as he made a joke about her singing. When their eyes finally connected, Rachel became so lost that she stopped moving. Naseem's warm hands on her waist was turning her on.

"You're so beautiful," Naseem said raising a hand to her face. Their lips connected and tongues dueled. Rachel moaned in submission as Naseem took charge.

"I'm tired of playing these games with you," said Rachel breaking the kiss briefly. She pulled Naseem to a private area. On a bench, she pulled off his jacket; kissing him with all passion and built-up frustration. Rachel wanted the sparks, flames, intensity, thrill, and him right now. She pulled his hair as she kissed while unable to figure out what is it about him that drove her so crazy. She'd could only imagine what it would be like when they were alone in bed.

"I want you, habibtee," said Naseem with a subtle bass in his voice.

Rachel wanted nothing more but to surrender and end this little game of theirs, but there were a few more lessons she had to teach him first. She pushed him back. Naseem was shocked as Rachel kissed him over and over as she kept going down.

"Mmmm." She moaned as she started unbuttoning his top button.

"I'd love nothing more than to give in to you." Rachel began saying in her sexiest tone as she rubbed his chest."But your brother, I fear he's in love with me and will not let me go without a fight."

"He'll get over it." Naseem said as he moved his hands were down to her hips; caressing her curves.

"I'm not so sure about that." She said, putting her hands over his. "He told me tonight he'll make me a very rich woman if I agree to marry him."

"I have more than him."

"He said I can work in the lab, and that he'll always be loving and dutiful."

"I can build you a lab and do both. What else?"

"He said he won't take any wives after me."

"Well, I—."

"I've found what I wanted."

Naseem started fondling Rachel's breast causing her to gasp. When he brushed his tongue over her lips, she opened them willingly. As his hands began lifting her dress, she pushed him back.

"Or mistresses."

"I don't want anyone else at this time."

"Now, what can he offer you that I cannot?"

"Hmm, I don't know. No one can compete with a sultan, can they, Naseem?" Rachel whispered sexily in his ear.

"No, they cannot." Naseem said now realizing Rachel trapped him.

"I knew it! I knew it!" Rachel got up poking Naseem in the chest.

"How long have you known?" Naseem looked like a schoolboy in trouble.

"Let's just say not long."

Naseem looked so sexy when he looks like this. Focus Rachel, you're angry with him, remember.

"Why did you lie?"

"I—I didn't know if I could trust—"

"That's funny. You didn't know if you could trust me. But I'm the one who was kidnapped her for you?"

"I had no idea my mother would stoop to such levels of desperation. I also didn't know what role you were playing in this until they told me the truth. I was angry and could have ended it there."

"So why didn't you?"

"This." Naseem gestured. "This attraction between us. You can't deny neither can I."

Rachel sighed. "But you didn't have to lie to me, Naseem."

"The crazy thing is I trusted you. You made me feel good. I'm scared, you know. I miss my family and the one person I trusted, broke that." Rachel tried holding back her tears.

"I will not force you to stay. If it is your wish to go, no one will stop you. I will personally see to it."

"And please don't think ill of my mother, she's under pressure. I mean a lot."

"How come?"

"There is a rule in our lands. If the heir to the throne is unmarried, he must be married by his 25th birthday with hopes of bearing heirs. If the heir cannot find a bride, the throne will then transfer to the first cousins of the royal family, The Amini Abdallah."

"And this is bad thing?"

"The Amini's have tried to wrestle control away from our family for centuries. They are a ruthless clan and mustn't have the throne."

Rachel looked up at the sky. "If there is one thing I've learned in life, it is that fear makes people do desperate things." Rachel said massaging his arm. "I will not hold this against Atiya. In a way, I understand and she and everyone here have been nothing but good to me. I get it. The fear of losing everything your ancestors have built is frightening. I cannot say if I would have done the same."

"Will you leave then?"

Naseem felt vulnerable. The last thing he wanted was for Rachel to know his family's ulterior motive.

"I really don't know," said Rachel shrugging.

Rachel finally had the easy out she wanted but the question now was, "Did she want to leave?"

"Please let me know what your decision is by week's end." Naseem stood up prepared to leave.

"You would marry me?" Rachel asked, looking him in the eyes.

"Without question."

"Why? That's crazy! I could be a serial killer."

Naseem had no answer.

"Why? You?" asked Rachel again.

"You're smart and got some wit. You challenge me when no one else would ever think to do so but you also do what is asked when necessary."

"Go on," said Rachel blushing.

"Did I mention you are a complete handful?"

"Ok and..."

"And you are beautiful. I'm glad we met even if it was because of my mother."

"Atiya is lovely. You're lucky to have her as a mother." Rachel rested her hand on his chest.

"I know."

"Stay, habibtee."

"Why should I?" Rachel said with a hint of playfulness as she smiled. She liked the fact of Naseem begging.

"Because you want to."

That caused Rachel to blush.

"Naseem is so corny," she thought.

Naseem began to move in to kiss her again.

"Not so fast, prince. I'll stay but if only you will agree to my terms."

"Only if they are within my abilities."

"I still get to work in the lab, right?"

"Ok, but Rafiq will be with you."

"How long before your next birthday?"

"Six months."

"Ok, If you want to have me as your wife, you must convince me by your birthday."

"Done." Naseem said once again moving closer.

"You also have to give me my space. Let me earn my own money and do things that I want to do."

"Ok. Anything else?"

"No sex."

Naseem turned away. Rachel could have sworn she heard him growl.

"And I want a firs-class ticket back home if I ask. If you lie to me again, I will leave without thinking twice."

"Is that all?" Naseem asked grinding his teeth.

"Yes, now come here boy and give me my kiss."

Rachel opened her heart hoping she made the right decision.

CHAPTER EIGHT

Meanwhile outside of the ballroom…

*H*aithum and his mother embraced each other as Fadil looked disappointed.

"Oh, cheer up Ibnee, she was never yours to begin with." Atiya held up her youngest son's chin.

"We must hurry with the wedding preparations. With our luck, they'll be married by the beginning of khareef."

"The girl didn't say she would marry him yet," said Fadi still disappointed.

"Look at them, my sons. Of course, they will."

It has been 3½ weeks since Rachel said she would give Naseem a chance. Right after their agreement, she began working with a group of researchers on a new drug that could help people with multiple sclerosis. She was the lead assistant for running the tests.

As Rachel loaded the samples into the GC-MS, she thought back onto how things had evolved between her and Naseem. Staying true to his word, Naseem allowed her to work regular hours while being paid. Meanwhile, her bodyguard Rafiq was always on standby.

While at work, Rachel discovered that Naseem's favorite color was purple, he traveled to over 100 countries, and his favorite time of the day was at sunset. Rachel and Naseem also had shared interests of R&B, Italian food, and watching Netflix.

Rachel looked up at the clock on the wall, it was after 5:30 and she was supposed to leave thirty minutes ago. Rafiq usually came in to remind her but not today. Rachel set the GC to run the samples overnight and rushed onto the elevator. She was pissed at Rafiq who was waiting outside the door looking at his cell phone.

"Why didn't you tell me it was past five? You know Naseem will have my head if I'm late for dinner," Rachel said as the elevator doors opened.

"I'm sorry, my lady. I didn't want to disturb."

When they reached the car, Rachel began fidgeting. As part of the agreement, Naseem had insisted on them having dinner together. Sometimes, Rachel would cook and other times, the servants. The dinners were private and Naseem would regularly pick out something sexy for her to wear. Like a dress with jewels attached and matching heels. The garments would at her door, gift-wrapped but that changed when Rachel came in late. Naseem shocked her having had her entire wardrobe brought downstairs. Then, he made Rachel change until he was finally pleased. She ended up wearing a black-fitted dress that came just went past her knees and had small oval cuts under the breast area. The dress was so tight, Rachel couldn't wear a bra underneath.

The second time she was late, Naseem had picked something from her American wardrobe; a short black cheerleader dress that had mesh cutouts around her upper breasts and lower stomach. If that wasn't bad enough, Naseem also picked out the bra and panties and insisted she serve him dinner while sitting on his lap.

Naseem always tried rubbing Rachel's thighs up to her pussy if her attire was short. It was his way of punishing her for being late and she actually liked it but she would stop him when reached a certain point.

"No sex," she said. "Remember."

When it was third time Rachel was late, she arrived and hurried inside. Checking the clock at the entrance, she sighed. It read 5:59 and dinner was always at six. She stared at Rafiq and he just shrugged.

Naseem walked in on them after ending a business

call and Rachel licked her lips in anticipation. Rafiq quickly exited the room. Naseem came and embraced Rachel.

"You're late again," Naseem said smiling while his hands went close to her booty and Rachel moved them downward.

"So what, prince. What are you going to do to me."

Rachel kissed his cheek and tried freeing herself from his grip and he stopped her.

"I assume my clothes are at the door for tonight?"

"You're correct." Naseem tried kissing her and Rachel ducked. She tried even though she enjoyed them.

"Ass," mumbled Rachel when Naseem eventually let her go. She was leaving to go to her room to shower when Naseem called out.

"Make sure you don't take too long. I'm hungry."

"Don't tell me what to do, boy. I'm not your slave."

Rachel showered for 20 minutes and then took another fifteen oiling herself down. When she went to get her clothes, she found a black corset with see-through shorts along with black lacey panties that had pink straps. In a second pile, there was thigh-high pantyhose and a pair of 6-inch pumps. All her attire was chosen from her American wardrobe. In between the piles, a note was left stating: "Come late more often."

Rachel laughed. "There's no way I'm wearing this." She checked her closets and drawers and found they were empty.

"Fucking smart ass." Rachel sighed feeling like she lost.

She got dressed and called for Hibba to come help her do her makeup and something with her hair. After another twenty minutes, Rachel was ready to go. Rafiq had escorted her and left without her noticing.

It was especially quiet this evening. Normally, Rachel saw the palace staff prepping for tomorrow but today no one was around.

What's this boy up to now?

When Rachel got to the dining room, she couldn't help but smile. There were candles all around and instead of dinner, there were plates of small pastries, fruits, chocolates, ice cream, syrups and whipped cream. Naseem was standing in front with a briefcase on the table.

As the doors closed behind her, Rachel thought,"Let the games begin."

"You look wonderful tonight," said the prince as he looked Rachel up and down.

"Thanks, habibi."

"Call me Nimr for this evening."

"What's its meaning, my prince?"

"Tiger."

"Good evening, Nimr. How may I serve you this evening?"

Rachel was upset that Naseem had won, but she loved playing these games with him. She wanted to push him down on the table, crawl on top and fuck the shit out him once and for all.

"No sex, remember girl," Rachel thought.

Naseem smiled as Rachel slowly began walking towards him, glamorizing her movements. When she was near, he pulled her in and this time, Rachel didn't resist. There was no pretense as this was their time to take care of business. Naseem began kissing her and Rachel exchanged fluids with him. His hands were on her booty as he slipped his tongue in and out.

"Oh, Nimr." Rachel moaned when he French-kissed her.

"Now, you can start by putting two of everything on a plate." Naseem smacked her butt as Rachel headed to the stove. Naseem took off his suit jacket and sat down at the head of the table. Rachel did what he asked and sat down on his lap to feed him. As he bit, she bit and Rachel felt his dick bulging within his pants.

"I got him," she thought.

"How was work today, honey?"

Rachel rubbed his chest and continued feeding him.

"All went well. I negotiated a few new deals in Europe, and expanded our line into the Phillipines." Nasem began rubbing Rachel's arm up and down.

"So the usual then?"

"Yes, the usual as you Americans all say."

"What did you do today?"

"Well, I put the finishing touches on the trial one drug, and then I—" Rachel began but abruptly cut off as Naseem pecked the left side of her neck. He looked at her playfully and she continued.

"...began analysis on the samples. We have to make sure, Mmmm..." She moaned as he continued pecking.

"Go on." He said as he suck down and began pecking on a path lower.

"We have to make sure, we know everything about the samples before we...Ahh...start testing them with patients." Rachel without knowing pushed her chest up higher. By then, Naseem had pulled out Rachel's left breast and was now slowly licking around her areola. He then placed her at the edge of the table clutching both breasts now.

"Mmmm...and I also...mmmm...I also went on a lunch picnic," said Rachel between gasps as she grabbed his hair.

"A lunch picnic?" Naseem said confused not seeing a company picnic on the schedule.

"Yes...with Fadi." Rachel moaned and gasped as Naseem had just bitten her left nipple.

"How's my little brother doing, anyway?" Naseem asked putting her breasts back inside her shirt.

"Still in love, still the charmer and romantic. What a man!" Rachel laughed.

Naseem ignored her and went back to his place at the table.

"I think I'll keep having lunch with him. I do have to keep my options open, right?"

"Shut up and don't move," Naseem said while he opened his briefcase. Rachel felt something soft wrap around her ankles but thought nothing of it. She was so caught up talking she hadn't noticed what Naseem was doing. When Rachel moved, she realized her ankles were chained. She gasped feeling so vulnerable. They stared into each other's eyes.

"So you want this work, huh?"

"You mean I'm at work."

"Whatever."

"Let me go."

"No. You're being a bad girl."

"I am?"

"Yes, you are."

Did Rachel want him some? She really wanted to lose her virginity, but did it matter when?

"Come kiss me." Rachel said as she pulled Naseem down on top.

As their lips and tongues clashed, they moaned

together. Rachel unbuttoned Naseem's shirt and grabbed his abs as she kissed.

"You need to learn how to reciprocate," she whispered.

With both naked from the waist up, Naseem instructed her to lay back once again. He began trying to find her spot as she ran her hands through his hair.

"Mmm...that feels so good daddy," She moaned as he sucked and bit down on her nipples. His hands held her breasts firmly. His tongue swagged around the outer rim of her right areola and worked his way inward. Rachel arched back and moaned as he licked it back and forth. The dark area being sucked and his wet tongue gave Rachel convulsions. She scratched his back and it made Naseem sucked harder.

"Oh, daddy." Rachel held her right breast in his mouth as if she was breastfeeding. Naseem licked her puffy nipple and then down. Then, a bit lower to her stomach.

After that, he stared; waiting for confirmation.

As soon as they made eye contact, he slowly began pulling down her shorts.

Oh my God! I'm letting him do this. What the fuck!

Rachel couldn't resist and tried opening her legs but remembered the fur and leather cuffs.

"You got me."

"I know."

Rachel kept moaning as Naseem kissed around

her inner thighs. She opened her legs as wide as she can as he went down further. As much as Naseem enjoyed this, he was ready to taste Rachel's pussy. He raised her buttocks and pulled her towards his mouth. Rachel winced as he began licking. Naseem had never done so before but wanted to now. Naseem split Rachel's lips and gulped. They moaned as he kept licking around it in a clockwise motion. Rachel was indeed caught in a rapture.

"Fuck." Rachel gripped Naseem's hair knocking off his keffiyeh.

"You like that."

"Yes, Tiger, I love it. Oh my God! It feels so fucking good." Naseem put his finger inside.

"Oooooh, daddy." Rachel moaned as she began to moving in sync with Naseem's finger and then he put in a second.

After two minutes of this sweet torture, she begged him for more as she came on his hand.

"Tiger—?" Rachel said barely able to breathe.

"I'm here."

"I need—"Rachel stopped and licked her lips. She changed positions causing her breasts to jiggle.

"What is it my love?"

"I want…ooooo…" She moaned as he began sucking her nipples again.

"What is it you want?" Naseem started fingering her again but more a bit slower.

"I—I—(Rachel kept moaning)…Tiger, fuck me!"

She ended as she jumped from the orgasms Naseem was giving her.

Naseem moved back on top of her and continued to playing with her clit as they french-kissed. Rachel hurriedly undid his belt and unzipped his pants. Naseem's dick was rock hard and she jerked it up and down. When Rachel moved closer to position him right at her opening, he followed, rubbing his head against her clit. This caused his dick to become harder and Rachel moaned, squirming trying to get Naseem to put it inside her. Naseem was about to put it in.

Then, there was a knock.

CHAPTER NINE

*N*aseem continued to rub her clit and yelled,"Maadah?"

"I'm sorry to disturb you Sayyidi, but fee muskila with one region." Rafiq said outside the door.

"In the North?" He asked growling. Rachel was silently moaning as she rubbed her pussy juice all over his dick.

"Nam, Sayyidi."

"Mautana?" He asked holding his dick and placing his finger inside making Rachel moan.

"Me-ah, so far Sayyidi."

"Have everyone meet in the conference room in five."

"Nam, Sayyidi." Rafiq went away.

"I have to go but—"

"It's okay, baby. I know you're busy but don't get hurt!"

"I have five minutes." Naseem moved down, so he was at Rachel's opening.

"Naseem, Oooo!" Rachel yelled as he once again parted her lips with his tongue, swirling it around her juices. After a few licks, he stopped at her clit and began sucking in and out.

"Oh my—!" Rachel bounced up and down on his tongue and continued wiggling. Naseem slowly put his finger in and out.

"I don't want...I don't want to cum without you in me, baby." Rachel pleaded.

Naseem continued sucking. With each suck, it took Rachel closer to climaxing. Her muscles tensed up as Naseem continued going; getting her closer and closer.

"Naseem...Naseem...Naseem!" She squealed as he stroked faster.

"Fuck, Naseem—Tiger--" Rachel screamed and shaked as an orgasm overtook over her body. She moaned as he continued licking until the tremors subsided. Rachel grabbed Naseem's face and kissed him, swapping. Their eyes were flashing with emotion, as she licked over his beard. He undid the cuffs at her ankles and Rachel wrapped her legs around him.

"That was so unfair."

"But, you enjoyed every second of it."

Naseem put on his shirt and Rachel buttoned it and then fastened his belt. Naseem kissed her again and walked to the door.

"Tell your mother I'm picking out my own dress."

"Are you sure?"

She nodded and smiled. Naseem came back pushing Rachel down, and grinding on her as their tongues dueled. Rachel grabbed his cock and Naseem was about to say "hell with the uprising and let's finish what we started."

"I must go." Naseem stepped back putting on his suit jacket. Rachel licked her lips and fingers watching him walk away. "Damn boy!"

CHAPTER TEN

*R*achel walked back to her bedroom dazed. She closed her door and rest on it as her mind wandered about getting some dick. Once she showered, she decided to do a little research on the so-called uprising and check her email. After her agreement, Rachel was given the log-in for the laptop. She typed Omash in Google and scrolled down until she found a webpage titled the History of the Mighty Omash. The article read:

The Al Said Hamaad's have ruled Omash as a monarchy since its first sultan, Ghazi Haad Al Said Hamaad came to power in 1281. Ghazi Haad Al Said Hamaad also known as 'Ghazi the Wise' established Omash after the The Battle of Laheya. During the Battle of Laheya, Ghazi and the eight clans overthrew the oppressive Gudayan regime. Ghazi was declared ruler and the eight clans divided themselves into 4 regions. The Humaidi, Awaan, and Ash-Sheikh occupied the Northern mountainous region. The Adab and Ma'el were the rulers of the Southern tropics. The Isin were of the Western deserts and the Imitti and Eshtar ruled the Eastern coastal lands. Rachel then searched: conflict in northeast Omash. There was not much news on the actual conflict but she saw numerous reports of strife between the Awaan and Imitti.

Rachel then signed into her email and Twitter account. A few weeks ago, she updated her status letting her family and close friends know she was staying in Omash for a wonderful work opportunity. Most wrote back wishing her well and saying she would be missed. Rachel also had a private message from her roommate telling her some pretty hot Arab guys came by to get her belongings and gave her money for the rest of their lease. Rachel responded:

My employers are pretty serious. They're so rich that as soon as they interviewed me for the job, they sent for me right away. I'm sorry to run out on you and Louie. I miss you both. At my new workplace, I'm working on the synthesis of a drug to assist in the curing MS. Wish me luck!

Rachel then went to check her emails. There was nothing unusual except a message from her mother. It read:

Dear Rachel,

I have not heard from you in a long time and your mother misses you. I know that you and I have not always seen eye to eye for years but you are my daughter and I love you. Your brothers told me you have some new job overseas somewhere. I wish you would have stopped by to see me before you left but I understand. My little girl has grown up; she's a grown woman now and living her life. If you get a break, you know how to reach me and you know where I will be. Live your life and be happy my child. I will always love you no matter what.

— FOREVER & ALWAYS, MARY.

Rachel didn't know what to write her mother. Although, they weren't on the best of terms, she didn't hate her. She thought it would be best to talk to Atiya later and ask her advice on the matter. She closed the laptop and went to Naseem's office. When she arrived, he was visibly worn out standing at the door holding his head.

"You didn't say goodnight, baby."

"Goodnight, my lady."

Naseem went back inside leaving the door open. He sunk into his chair and sat back with his eyes closed; facing the ceiling.

"Poor thing, you look so tired."

"Wallah, I am."

"Let me help then." She said locking the door behind and walking over. Naseem thought she was going to give him a massage but was shocked when he opened his eyes to find her kneeling before him. Rachel unfastened his belt and pulled his dick out; looking him directly in the eyes.

"Rachel—"

"Don't—" She cut him off, "This is reciprocation." She kissed his head and started licking around it. Then, she put it into her mouth, wetting its length. Rachel was shy about doing this as this was her first time. She pushed Naseem backward and bobbed up and down. When his dick was wet enough, she grasped it jerking up and down as she sucked. Naseem could only grab both sides of the chair.

The foreplay started off light and then increased as Rachel became more used to it. She went up and down and looked Naseem in the eyes as she kept going. She bobbed up and down; hitting his sensitive spots. Naseem grabbed her head and pushed it down. "Mmm!" Rachel said tasting Naseem was about to cum. All the sudden, he got up and walk over to his desk.

"Come here and bend over."

Rachel got up confused. She spread her legs wanting him to insert. Naseem turned her around with her ass up and braced himself. He rubbed his dick on both sides of her pussy walls causing Rachel to call him daddy. Seconds later, she looked back shockingly; feeling Naseem's cum on her ass.

"That was dirty," pouted Rachel.

"Yeah, I know," said Naseem grabbing a tissue and wiping it off her.

"No sex before marriage, remember?"

"But—you wanted some."

"And you did too, but the rules are the rules."

Rachel stared at him thinking,"two can play this game." She shoved him as she fixed her clothes.

"Goodnight, Rachel," chuckled Naseem.

"Goodnight, ass."

"Will you always call me that when you're angry?"

"Yes, because you are one," said Rachel folding her arms. Through her shirt, you could see her nipples were rock hard.

Naseem licked his lips as he looked at them.

"Goodnight, ass. Like I said."

Rachel left and Naseem stood there shaking his head.

CHAPTER ELEVEN

*T*he next day Rachel awoke to a bustle of activity. She heard servants walking back and forth, talking. She dressed and walked to the front, finding Naseem on a business call. Rachel slowly approached as he ended.

"What's going on, honey?"

"I'm traveling to the Northeast to attempt a cease fire."

"Sounds like a good idea, I'll take the second Mercedes then."

"No, you will not. The guards will be monitoring the palace and protecting you until I get back. There could an attack and I want you to be safe."

"There will be no safer place than being with you." Rachel walked over and caressed his face. "Besides, if I'm your wife to be, I will be by your side at all times. Trust me."

"But—"

"No buts, I'm not one of those Arab chicks you can just fuck as you like and leave." Rachel began whispering, so the guards wouldn't overhear their conversation. "I refuse to be a pretty little housewife waiting for you, cooking you dinner, getting fucked at night and then you leave me for the rest of the day."

Naseem's eyes sparked when she said the word *"fuck."* It brought back flashbacks to when they almost did some hours ago.

"Yes, I know we will both do our own thing but marriage is a partnership, boo. I'm not just signing on to be your wife, I'll be their queen and a damn good one."

Rachel and Naseem stared into each other's eyes.

"Tayyib," said Naseem. Rachel gave herself an applause.

"But you must obey my rules and don't attempt to get in the middle of anything or go off on your own. Rafiq and Hamid be everywhere you are, understood?"

"Understood, my prince."

Rachel gave Naseem a quick kiss and went off to the Mercedes.

Rachel rode with Rafiq, Hamid and Hibba behind Naseem and his guards. As they drove to the region which was nearly two hours away, Rachel thought over what Naseem said and had no idea what the hell was going on. When they arrived, a foul odor appeared. Rachel looked seeing rows and rows of the dead bodies wrapped in white shrouds near the gate of the city. Maha handed Rachel a niqab and she put it on before stepping out. The leaders of both sides agreed to a truce for a day to talk with Naseem and were waiting for him a tent in the center of a makeshift encampment. Naseem went to Rachel first and grabbed her hands. "You can't go in there with me. I will listen to both parties and I promise to tell you everything that is happening and what I will do." "Don't leave Rafiq and Hamid's sight."

"Ok. Come back to me in one piece." Rachel squeezed his hand as she looked at the heavily armed men outside of the tent.

Naseem entered the tent with two men and after greeting one another, they sat.

"The losses are heavy on both sides. This fighting will solve nothing but costing more lives. You will leave wives without husbands, and fathers without sons. We must find a way to end this today. What is the cause of this senselessness?" The two men began talking at the same time. "Stop! I'm here to listen and help but nothing can be solved with both of you yelling." Naseem gestured to the man on the left, the leader of the Imitti clan to speak first.

Outside of the tent, Rachel wandered around and

saw many women and children peeking out of tents looking fearful. She went over to an old woman and greeted her as Maha translated.

"The woman says you have clothes befitting a queen." Hibba said and Rachel thanked her.

"There are rumors in the lands, my dear, that the sultan has taken a wife. Are you her? " Hibba continued.

"I will be," Rachel said extending her hand. Rachel's words shocked Maha. " The woman excitedly made the ululation along with others present.

"Why are all the women here, so close to the fighting?" Rachel asked.

"To care for the dead and sick." Maha translated. Rachel thanked the woman and continued touring. A group of women now followed her as she went around assessing the conditions. Children from both sides were running through the garbage. Rachel noticed what appeared to be a stream coming from the mountains and walked closer. She saw a young boy alone, watching the children as he sat with a dog that was panting of thirst.

"Maha, ask our new friend his name and why is he sitting alone watching the others?" The group of women present made faces and looked angry as Maha spoke.

"He's a yateem (which means orphan my lady)

and the villagers want nothing to do with him. He was left behind by the other side."

"Where are his parents and family?" Rachel asked observing him.

"He has no family," a woman said. "They were told his mother died in childbirth and his father was a drunken fool who fell to his death."

"What happens to the orphans here?" asked Rachel.

When Hibba didn't answer, Rachel looked back at the women and saw they looked uncomfortable. Rachel then looked back at Hibba.

"Most die or wander off somewhere."

"Why doesn't some others take them in?"

"They can barely take care of themselves."

Rachel was torn between anger and sadness.

"You have to understand my lady, that's the way it has always been for centuries."

Rachel noticed the boy had a sling around his arm. "How did he get hurt?"

"He was--kicked trying to save that dog during a village protest," one woman answered.

"How could this happen?" Rachel sighed then slowly approached the boy. She saw him feeding the dog a piece of bread and trying to coax it into drinking some water. "Hello, my name is Rachel , what's yours?" Maha interpreted but the boy spoke English.

"I'm Rayan."

Rachel was startled he spoke in English.

"My father taught me English words before he died. He was a brave man," Rayan said kicking around the dirt.

"How long has it been since your father passed?" Rachel asked gently as she kneeled.

"Two...three years."

Rachel frowned; angry to think that this small child could be on his own. "It's very nice to meet you Rayan, and who is our friend here? I heard you saved her, that was very brave of you. What kind of dog is it?"

"I have not named her yet and she's a Saluki."

"Rayan..."Rachel began unexpectedly. "How would you like a job?"

"What kind of job, my lady?"

"Please, just call me Rachel and the job is being my royal translator. I don't know Omashi and my current teacher is horrible."

Rayan perked up and came closer.

"I think I can help you while you teach me Omashi. Does that sound like a deal?" asked Rachel

"Sounds good, Rachel. But how will I help you? I live here."

"Well, since you will be my royal translator, you'll have to stay in my palace. Close enough to where I need you. You and your saluki can have your own room."

Rayan jumped up and gave her a hug. Rachel

held him tight hoping her tears wouldn't fall. She still needed Naseem's okay. Rachel also did not want this to happen ever again to the children.

"You have to make me a promise before I agree, Rayan. You have to promise to go to school every day before our lessons, ok? Education is key."

"Ok, Rachel, I promise." Rayan said embracing her.

"Now, I want you to follow Hibba and go get anything you have and wait for me at my car, okay."

"Ok."

"I'll see you in a bit," said Rachel ruffling his hair.

The women were shocked as they saw the boy race off. One woman voiced her opposition loudly. "What is she saying, Rafiq?" Rachel asked.

"The women's asking why did you that. She says he's a dirty son of a fool."

"Tell her: There's no such thing as a dirty son because he comes from the other side. We are one community and must learn to work together. We'll never have anything if we continue to fight."

Meanwhile, Naseem exited the tent and had gotten both sides to agree to continue the cease fire. As a result, he would return in a few days with a long-term proposal. He watched Rachel shaking the hands of the women as the children ran around smiling.

"What has this woman done?" He asked one of his guards.

"She's taken an orphan boy and is talking to the women about working together."

"An orphan?" Naseem said shockingly.

"Ajaal, your majesty." The guard gestured toward Rayan who was running back to Rachel. Naseem watched as she crouched down and spoke. While they were talking, Naseem approached them.

"Rachel."

"Your majesty," the boy responded.

"I'd like you to meet our new Royal translator. I wish for him to teach me Omashi if it so pleases you."

"Your Amiri, I'm Rayan. I will be your new royal Translator and protectior to Amira Rachel if Allah wills.“

"Protector? That is a big job, are you sure you can handle it, my boy?”

Rayan nodded.

"Even it's a big one for men like me?" Naseem said, towering over him.

"Yes, sir, I will do my best,“ Rayan said, standing up straight.

Naseem looked him up and down as Rachel bit her lips nervously in silence. "Well, in that case, you're hired."

Rayan ran back to the car and Rachel and Naseem walked slowly behind as their guards and the rest flanked.

"Thank you, my prince. How can I show you I care?"

"I'm sure you'll think of a way." Naseem smiled at her suggestively. "You have a good heart, Rachel."

"So do you but you just try to hide it."

Night fell as the group drove home, and Rayan chatted excitedly with Rachel about how he would be the best Royal Translator and bodyguard she could ask for. After a while, he fell asleep; his little head fell onto Rachel 's lap. Rachel stared outside the window as her mind wandered. "Stop the car." She yelled abruptly and the car came to a screeching halt. Rachel carefully moved Rayan over and stepped out, going to what had caught her attention. Naseem got out asking, "What is she doing?"

"She said she's never seen a waterfall before."

"Wait here." Naseem removed his jacket and tie before going after Rachel. Rachel was already at the passage, lifting her dress and slowly stepping knee-deep into the beautiful blue-green waters. She sat on a rock and listened to the rushing water as she faced the star-filled sky.

"Do they not have waterfalls in America?" Naseem asked sarcastically; removing his shoes and getting in the water.

"Can I tell you something without you laughing at me?"

"I promise not to laugh."

"I didn't know things like this existed here. I thought it was all desert."

Naseem let out a loud laugh.

"Hey, ass," Rachel said splashing water on him.

"The thoughts you Americans have of us. Get in the water with me."

"But I'll get wet."

"You're always wet."

Rachel tied her dress around her mid-thighs and stepped inside.

"Tell me about the war these people are having." She put her arms around Naseem.

"They are fighting over resources. The Awaan have a stream that runs through the mountain, so they have access to fresh water and a lot of vegetables. The Imitti have the coastal area, and here they grow garlic, onions, spinach, squash and celery."

"Do they harvest during the same season?" Rachel asked running her hands through Naseem's hair.

"No, the Awaan have a short harvest around the late summer and the Imitti's during the spring, fall and early summer."

"Well, begin there. They need to help one another during their off-seasons. If they do, they will both have more than enough crops and can trade for what they don't have. It is a win-win situation."

"The only problem is, they don't want to share."

"I was thinking that." She said holding him tightly make her dress rise higher. You have three options, honey.

Option 1: Force them to work together."

"Go on." Naseem said massaging her thighs.

"Option 2: Suggest they work together but not formally force them to do so.

Option 3: Lead by example and bridge the gap between both and show them how."

"Ok." Naseem began contemplating. "I agree with all you gave but I think the third is the easiest."

They were now out of the water and laying on the sand when Naseem pulled her down on top of him.

"Naseem!"

He silenced her with a hard kiss and Rachel immediately yielded.

"You'll make an excellent queen. You did well today."

"I like solving problems. Speaking of which there's still one," Rachel suggested grabbing his dick.

"No sex, remember." Naseem teased and Rachel gently pushed.

They laid that way for an half an hour as Rachel played in Naseem's hair while gazing at the stars.

"This is weird." Rachel said turning her head to the side.

"What?"

"If this was America, we'd be boyfriend and girlfriend."

"Girlfriend? I have never had one. There hasn't been much time for such things."

"But you know what you're doing with me?" "Yeah, right!"

"I'm learning the ropes."

"Lies!"

"I'm not."

"So, I know you want to marry me, right. But don't you think we should be like fiances first?"

"You mean engaged?"

"Yes, like that. It'll let everyone know I'm off the market."

"Is someone bothering you?"

"Not really besides Fadi." Rachel chuckled as she held his hand.

"I will let that little rascal know you are off the market."

"Don't beat him up."

"I won't."

CHAPTER TWELVE

A few days later, Atiya stopped by for the family's weekly Wednesday dinner.

"I'm glad you arrived early, we have a lot to talk about."

"Al hamdulilah, I heard you've been courting my son well." Atiya embraced Rachel; kissing her on her cheeks.

"I feel this is the right decision. I can help him and he can help me. We have the perfect life here in Omash." Rachel said looking at Rayan in the other room.

"I'm so glad you've come to your senses. Now, I don't want you to worry about anything. I'll take care of everything except the dress. We'll meet with the designer soon."

"Ok," Rachel said hinting sadness.

"My dear, what's wrong?"

"My mother wrote me and I don't know what to do."

"What happened?"

"Long story short. My father died when I was thirteen. He had a stroke behind the wheel. We were all devastated. After his funeral, his best friend helped us out a lot; took my brothers to football practice, helped me with homework, looked after my mom and etc." Rachel's eyes started tearing and Atiya reached over and grabbed her arm.

"Then, I caught that man and mom having sex one day after school. My father hadn't even been dead for a year yet and she was already moving on with his best friend."

"Ya, Allah! Sit, Bintee. I'll tell you something about my late husband. He's been gone for eleven years. There's not a day that goes by that I do not think of him. I see him every time I look at our amazing children we're blessed to have. I see him on these walls, the memories we shared, and the happiness we once had. That kind of love does not just go away. I still love him but after he passed I fell in love again."

"How?"

"The heart is a resilient organ. It can be damaged many times over and repaired. You think you will never get over its pains and then you simply do. The heart has the capacity for more than one love. I love my husband, and no matter who I love or who loves me after that, it will not undo anything that he and I ever had. I still have the utmost respect for his legacy, and I will never speak ill of him." Atiyah paused reflecting on her next words carefully. "If you open yourself up to the new man, it won't erase the memories you had with your father. Don't be afraid, Bintee. No one can ever replace him."

"I feel so guilty."

"Don't, your father would want you all to be happy. Let it go. Make amends with your mother. Your father would not be happy seeing you two fight like this. You are happy here with my son, are you?" Atiya held Rachel's hands.

"Yes, I am."

"Do you think your mother deserves that kind of happiness, as well?"

"You're right. How do you know so much?"

"Truth is, I don't. But that is our little secret."

"Okay."

"Now, please go and tell Naseem the food is ready."

Rachel wiped the tears as she walked to Naseem's office. He was asleep at his desk. She looked at him as awe overtook over her, stroking his hair and whispering in his ear, "I love you."

Rachel quietly left, closing the door and had dinner with Atiya and Rayan.

It took Rachel about a week to come up with the right reply to her mother's message. She sent it when she was on lunch and it read:

Dear Mother,

It's great to hear from you. Are you and Elliot doing well? I'm here in Omash working with a team to create a new drug for multiple sclerosis. I think Dad would be proud. After graduation, I got an unexpected offer from Hamaad LLC and couldn't pass up the offer. I'm sorry I didn't say goodbye. I left rather quickly without saying goodbye to anyone. This place makes me so happy. Mom, I have met someone that's special. My life is beginning to change for the better. We'll talk about it in person, one of these days.

— UNTIL THEN. MUCH LOVE,
RACHEL

Rachel hit "send" and let out a sigh of relief. She was about to return to her lunch when there was a knock. "Come in." Fadi walked in holding a vase.

"Good afternoon, Rachel . These are for you."

"Oh Fadi, you shouldn't have! You're so sweet."

"How are you?" They both asked at the same time.

"Go ahead, my love." Fadi said.

"Ok, then—" said Rachel was flabergasted

shaking her head. "Fadi, my research's going well despite a few hiccups here and there. Rayan's adjusting great in school. The other night we named his Saluki, Lanah." "Aside from that, I'm fine and your brother is still—How about you?"

"Well, I—"

"Fadi! What are you doing in here with my woman!?!" Naseem said walking in holding a small case.

"Naseem!" Rachel got up holding him.

"Ya Gabee!" Naseem said grasping Rachel's waist and was about to kiss her. He stopped and looked at his little brother. Fadi quickly left and Rachel rolled her eyes walking back to her seat.

"You know, some would call you possessive."

"Others would call me authoritative. I got you something." He opened a case revealing an oval diamond necklace and earrings that matched.

"A tad bit formal for the office, don't you think, Mr. Possessive?"

"Alright, alright. I see you have jokes."

Rachel turned around, so Naseem could put it on.

"It's a small thing, my lady."

"Well, I'm not really into flashy things, but this I like." Rachel stroked the necklace while giving Naseem a quick kiss.

"Well, I am glad you do."

Rachel posed in the office mirror suddenly thinking about what to get Rayan.

"Naseem."

"Nam!"

"How much did you pay for this?"

"Why?"

"I'm just curious." Rachel answered grinning.

"I see you're up to something."

"Please tell me, habeebee."

"About 450,000 deenars. Something small. It's your first engagement gift."

"Wow! I don't know how much is that in dollars but it sounds like a lot."

Naseem kissed her forehead and told Rachel she's worth the world.

"See you at home later, my love," Rachel smiled relishing the gift.

Naseem left and Rachel went back to lunch.

Naseem arrived home later that evening and found Rachel with Rayan in the dining room. He came up behind her and embraced her. "You'll spoil that boy. He isn't a child."

"He may be mature for his age but he's still a boy, Naseem." Rachel leaned back kissing him. "

When I was seven I—"

"You were a bad boy running around the palace naked. Your mother told me all the stories."

"By the way, I'm glad you're home because we have some things to discuss."

Naseem put his hand.

"Rachel, what do we need to discuss this late?"

"As you can see, I have a special interest in setting up programs for orphans and abandoned animals.

"Ok, sounds good. What do you need from me?"

"Just freedom to do this on my own for now, but let's move on to something else for a second. What's happening with my salary? I want to use that money to start something."

"I've been putting it in a special account for you."

"And you didn't say anything?"

"I got you as you say in your culture."

"That term is open for interpretation, ass."

"Hamid!" Naseem called out.

"Haadir, Sayyidi."

"Hamid, get all the bank documents for Rachel's account and take her to the bank manager first thing in the morning." Naseem then turned back to Rachel. "The bank manager will go over everything with you. I have to head out to the mountains early. Harvest season is coming soon and I'm taking your advice. I won't be home until late. If you have any questions, tell me at breakfast." Naseem kissed her on the forehead.

"Hamid."

Hamid appeared once again.

"Wait." Rachel said getting up. There's one more thing."

"What is it, my love?"

"Well, I want you to know that I really appreciate the gift you gave me earlier."

"Go on." Naseem waved Hamid away.

"So much so that I want to use it for something better."

"Laa!" Naseem answered.

"Lakin..."

"No buts. I'll see you in the morning. By the way, the coffee is getting much better. Keep up the good work." Naseem walked out.

"Shukran, honey." Rachel said in Arabic and Naseem smiled.

"You're learning our words already, I see."

"I've called the bank manager and he's waiting for us. Are you ready, my lady?" Hamid said knocking on Rachel's door early in the morning.

"Maha!" Rachel called out.

"Please make sure Rayan gets to school on time. Shukran!"

"Laa Mushkelah, Habibti!"

When Rachel and Hamid arrived at the bank, it was still closed. The manager unlocked the door and ushered them inside quickly.

"Rachel Johnson?"

"Yes."

"Right this way, Sayyida. You have three accounts with us. The first account ending in 1129 is your personal with weekly deposits of 5000 Riyals totaling 60,000 at the moment. The second ends in 1149 is deposited from Hamaad LLC totaling in 49,050 Riyals and the last ends in 1169 has one deposit of 15,000 Riyals."

"About how much in American dollars is 15,000 Riyals?" asked Rachel.

"Close to four thousand dollars."

"Shukran." Rachel replied staring at the numbers on the screen.

"Hamid, do you know anything about the third one?"

The bank manager excused himself.

"I believe, it's for your return to the United States just in case." The two conversed as the bank manager answered a call.

"Nam, Sayyidina. Heya hoona. Fee ghurfa thaniyah?" The bank manager said.

"Hadaa Naseem Al Said Hamaad." It was Naseem on the other line.

"Nam, Amiroona." said the bank manager with a slight stutter as he stood up straight out of respect.

"Ahteeha, khamsah mee-ah Alf edafa min kulli shay toreed," said Naseem.

"Tayyib, Amiroona. Marhaban," replied back the bank manager.

"Hayaakallah!"

"Wallahi Highyeek. Ateehaa, telephone min fadlik," requested Naseem.

"Ajaal, Sayyidina."

The bank manager informed Rachel that he had just been instructed by the sultan to give her an additional 500,000 Riyals and that he was waiting for her on the line.

"Shukran." Rachel said smiling as she walked to the phone.

"Yes. Salam alaykum."

"Wa alaykum as Salam. How are you my delicious, tasty future wife and queen?" Naseem said seductively, causing Rachel to blush.

"I'm good."

"What's that I hear in your voice?"

"I didn't like how we ended things earlier. You left so—"

"I don't say this often, but I'm sorry, habibtee. Sometimes I forget, we were raised in two separate cultures. I took offense to you wanting to use my gift for something else. There is no need to sacrifice. It's my job as your future husband. I'm willing to cater to your pleasure at your command."

Rachel put her hands over mouth before she answered. "So from this, you will give me anything that I want?"

"Yes, anything."

"I'll hold you to that," said Rachel seductively.

"I'll hold you to that, too."

"Yallah!"

"Masalama."

Rachel smiled as she walked back into the room with Hamid and the bank manager. "Please place 425,000 in the first account. I'd like to use the current balances of the first and second accounts to set up my charity fund."

"Ok, my lady."

"After August 25th, I want you to take all of the money out of the third and close the account. Put the money in a CD for the next 10 years for Rayan, with my name as co-owner on the account with 75,000 Riyal."

"Ok, Miss Johnson."

"Lastly, I want you to take this." Rachel removed her necklace and placed it in a safety deposit box. I'll be back to pick it up soon." She still wore the matching earrings.

"Hamid, do you happen to know the jeweler Naseem went to?" Before he could answer, the bank manager interjected.

"If I may, my lady. I believe the necklace was made by Ilmaas Majwahrat. They are an upscale jeweler that caters almost exclusively to the royal family."

"Great! I need to get another one made; one for a young boy."

"Say no more, my queen. I'll contact them right away if you please."

"Thanks so much. Please call right away."

"Laa Haraj."

Rachel and Hamid exited the building. "Hamid, I need you to take me to the State Office." Rachel said stepping inside the SUV.

"As you wish, my queen."

Once Rachel was finished at the State Office, she was happy to obtain Rayan's permanent residency.

"Thank you, Hamid. I'll be sure to make you some of my special fried chicken. You'll love my cooking." Rachel smiled getting back inside.

"No problem, my queen."

"May I share something else?" Rachel asked.

"As you wish.""It is weird hearing everyone call me Queen outside of being black. I'm barely used to the help I get at the palace and now everyone's bowing to me and taking care of everything I ask."

"It's our way of showing respect. We are very happy for the sultan. You'll make a fine Malika, Sayyida Rachel."

"I never imagined this ever happening. I'm so used to doing things on my own." "Hmm, by the way, can you take me to Naseem right now?"

"I don't know if the Sultan will approve this. It's not safe."

"Let me worry about Naseem. Take me home first, so I can change."

"As you wish."

When Rachel arrived back home, she found a blue and gold bag from Ilmaas Majwahrat on her bed. Inside were three satin pouches; the first was a bracelet with a note attached: *for you*, the second, was a gold chain, with a prayer in Arabic on a faceplate and a note which read: *for Rayan* and the third was a bracelet that matched the first but had the symbol of a man holding a sword. It was also for Rayan.

"I swear that man knows everything." She bundled all the jewelry and placed it inside her drawer. Rachel then quickly got dressed and headed off with Hamid.

CHAPTER THIRTEEN

*I*t was a few hours drive to the mountains and once Rachel and Hamid arrived, the sun was setting. Naseem and his men were coming from the harvest and he was dirty. He smiled as Rachel stepped out of the SUV. "Did you get my present?" Naseem asked while wiping his hands.

"I did and I have one for you. Do you like my trench coat?" Rachel said spinning around. The tan trench fitted her like a dress and exposed her long brown legs.

"I do, indeed." Naseem looked Rachel up and down.

"Good. I'll ride back with you while Hamid and the rest of the men can ride together," said Rachel walking back to his SUV.

"This girl's up to something?" thought Naseem as he

looked at Rachel getting inside and throwing her coat in the backseat.

"I'm glad you didn't reveal what's underneath to my man, Hamid." Naseem started the engine.

"This thing is for you, boo." Rachel kissed him as he pulled off.

After a few minutes of driving, there was a little distance between themselves and the others. Rachel turned and began putting her plan in motion, putting her hand down on Naseem's right thigh. "So how was work today, honey?"

"Things went well. No problems. At first, the Imitti weren't going to show up but as soon as they heard of my coming, they decided to come in bunches. They put the Awaan in charge and work got done without any issues."

While Naseem was talking, Rachel unzipped his pants and slid her hand in.

"That's good, baby." She looked ahead to see how close the other cars were. They were still far in front. Rachel then quickly unsnapped her seatbelt as she went down and started sucking Naseem's dick. She licked around the tip causing Naseem to lose focus.

"Oh my—Are you crazy?"

"Yes, I am." Rachel moaned at the taste of his cock inside her mouth. She started sucking slowly inch by inch trying her best. Naseem groaned and opened his legs wider. Rachel looked at him as she continued sucking while he was driving. Saliva was coming out of her mouth and Naseem was enjoying the moment. He put his hand on her head, guiding it up and down.

"Pay attention to the road, Naseem! Put both hands on the steering wheel." Rachel chuckled as she shook his hand off of her head. She went back down sucking harder; licking around the tip and flickering around the underside of his head before going back down on the base. Rachel swirled her tongue around the tip as Naseem groaned and gripped her head again bobbing her. His thighs thrusted as he started saying her name. She continued to move with him up and down, shaking his hand off her head once again. Up, down, up down, up down.

"Fuck I'm about to ---Rachel," Naseem yelled.

"Mmmm, are you baby?"

"This is it...oh shit!" Naseem sounded as he gripped the steering wheel as hard as he could. When Rachel felt the first of his cum coming out, she came up; grabbing his cock under the tip, preventing him.

"What the hell are you doing?"

"Do you want to cum for me, Naseem?" Rachel said loosening and then going back to lick in swirls around the top.

"Oh, oh!"

"Answer me." Rachel said continuing to tease him.

"Oh, hell yeah."

"Then all you have to do—" Rachel punctuated as she swirled her tongue,"is...pull over...and fuck the shit out of me."

Naseem gripped the steering wheel harder and gritted as he looked back and forth. He remembered what he said earlier but he still pulled over to the side of the road. Rachel bounced up from her seat and then stepped out. He stopped her. "Well—" Naseem began kissing her as she moaned while he ran his hands over her; squeezing her breasts and gripping her ass against the car door.

"But the first time we fuck, it will not be on the side of a dirt road," said Naseem breathing hard.

"Let's go fuck at home then."

"Let's go."

Rachel got back inside, put her seat belt back on and Naseem began driving again. He hit a button on the dashboard and Bashir's voice came through the speakers. "Nam, Sayyidi."

"Bashir, give the staff off for the night and inform my guards to keep distance from the private bedroom suites." Naseem had his arm on Rachel 's left thigh rubbing it.

"Ajal, Sayyidi."

When they drove through the palace gates, the guards kept their distance staying on the perimeter until Naseem and Rachel got out. They slowly entered behind. Rachel and Naseem raced to his bedroom and Rachel giggled when he smacked her on the butt. She was so excited that she finally won.

"I'm going to give it to him tonight," she thought as she opened his bedroom door. Rachel stood by the bed and Naseem prowled in behind. He unbuttoned his shirt and pulled his belt off. Rachel walked sexily to the head of the bed and turned toward him. She slowly unbuttoned the buttons on her trench coat and eased it off her shoulders. She was wearing a light blue and pink matching bra and thong with nothing else underneath. She turned, unhooking her bra and letting the thong down. Rachel then crawled onto the bed shaking her butt. Naseem looked at her, moving her ass up and down. It turned him on so he spanked her lightly, causing Rachel to jump.

You're so naughty." He said gripping a cheek. He bit on it before parting her lips and inhaling her pussy scent.

"Mmm," Naseem groaned as he took a long lick from the clit from behind. Her pussy odor was intoxicating. Rachel kept shaking her ass as Naseem flicked his tongue in and out, coaxing more juices.

"Naseem...fuuucck." Rachel slurred as she pushed back onto his tongue. After a few more licks, she turned around and started finger-fucking herself

much to Naseem's delight. She then pulled him down by his pants. She unfastened them and stroked his cock making him harder.

"Oh, that feels good." Naseem opened Rachel's legs wider and put his dick inside going in slowly. He stopped when he got to her hymen and looked at her. Rachel nodded and he pushed in further. Rachel held onto him and buried her face as she clenched the bed sheets from behind.

"Oh my—Fuck me—Fuck me!"

Since this was their first time having sex, Naseem wanted to take things slow. He sat back on his heels and lightly hit her pussy easing in and out in a light rhythm. Rachel moaned as Naseem began increasing the strokes hitting her G-spot. Her pussy was getting wetter and wetter, as Naseem stroked deeper and deeper.

"Fuck boy? Hit this harder. This is your pussy—" Rachel moaned. The feeling of him so deep inside was overly stimulating. Naseem continued stroking; with each, he played with her clit causing Rachel to moan louder. Rachel then wrapped her legs around him and began pumping in rhythm. They matched each other's and increased their tempos.

"Fuck! You're so wet." Naseem tried pulling out and slow down before he came.

"No, don't stop, I'm so close to—" said Rachel.

Naseem began stroking faster as Rachel played with her pussy moaning,"Naseem, Naseem, fuck, oh, Kingggggg--" She came screaming as her pussy muscles clamped around his dick.

"Oh my god!" Naseem said gritting as he released right after her.

Rachel stayed in position as Naseem was still ejaculating. She giggled as she started playing with his mustache. They kissed staying like that for a few minutes. Her unconsciously clamping and unclamping pussy muscles were vibrating while Naseem still kept cumming little by little inside her.

They tightly embraced as the calm settled. Rachel rubbed his back causing Naseem to get hard again. He got back on top of her and started stroking slowly.

"Oh, Naseem?" Rachel said trying to regain her composure.

"Hmm?"

"Do you...(click, click, click)... hear that?" she said arching as he continued hitting her G spot.

"No," he ignored her fondling her breasts.

"That's my wet pussy making that sound."

"Oh, my!" Naseem spread her legs wider.

"Fuck! Fuck! Fuck!" Rachel held his back while he kept penetrating deeper and deeper.

"You like that?"

"Yes-oh-daddy. Keep going prince. It feels so good." Rachel exhaled as she continued holding Naseem.

Before Naseem could make her cum again, they heard a series of loud noises and then crying.

CHAPTER FOURTEEN

*N*aseem and Rachel looked at each other puzzled before they sprang up. "It came from Rayan's room." Naseem said grabbing and buttoning up his pants.

"Are we under attack? Ya Allah! We sent the guards away for the evening." Rachel ran to grab her trench coat.

"Wait here," said Naseem but Rachel stubbornly ran behind him. Naseem grabbed a sword from the wall and pulled Rachel behind him as they walked to Rayan's room. When they got closer, Rachel ran around Naseem to find Rayan on the floor with a cup of spilled milk and Lanah licking it up.

"Rayan, what the hell just happened?" Rachel checked his arm which was still in a cast.

"I had a nightmare, my queen, so I went to the

kitchen to get a cup of milk. I tried getting back in bed when I knocked it over."

Meanwhile, a shirtless Naseem waved off the incoming guards as Rachel helped Rayan stand up.

"What was this nightmare about, honey?"

"There was a monster inside the palace. It was watching you and the sultan. It was saying some bad things."

"Ok. Let's get you some more milk. I'll tuck you in for bed for tonight."

"Ok." Rayan rubbed his little eyes.

"You see Naseem, over there?" Rachel pointed. Rayan nodded. "He's strong and fearless, and we are the most precious things to him. He will protect us from anything scary." "A few days ago, he protected me from the scariest monster, I've ever seen," said Rachel dramatically as she poured a glass of milk. She rubbed his head as he drank. "You want me to tell you what it was?" Rachel asked as they walked back to his room. Rayan nodded. "It was very big." She raised her hands and made a scary face. "And it had two big eyes." Rachel said moving toward him. "Aaand...eight legs!" she said excitedly as she began tickling him.

Rachel tucked Rayan in bed, kissed his forehead and said, "Goodnight."

"Goodnight, Queen." He answered half-sleep. Rachel grasped and squeezed Naseem's hands as they looked on.

Meanwhile, an unknown figure covered his face and turned away after watching them. Walking silently, he left the palace under the cloak of the night.

A few days later, Rachel received a response from her mother. It read:

Rachel,

It warms your old mother that you have written me back. Elliot and I are dong well. He makes me so happy. Your brothers are doing good. I'm sure you keep up with them on that social media. Hamaad LLC? I researched this on the internet and see that the headquarters is there where you are in Omash. That is very far. You've met someone, huh? When's the wedding and when will you be giving me grandchildren? I'm kidding. I miss you. Your father would be as proud as I am.

— KEEP SHINING BABY AND KEEP
IN TOUCH. LOVE, MOM.

Rachel wanted to email her back but trotted off to the kitchen first. She saw Atiya, Maha, Hibba and the maids all preparing dinner. Grabbing an apron Rachel said,"How can I help?"

"Actually, you're coming with me," said Naseem walking in.

Rachel was stunned seeing Naseem in a dark blue Tom Ford suit paired with a white dress shirt and dark blue shoes. "We're going out for a bit," said Naseem pulling Rachel. "Omi, I'll have us back before dinner."

"Khair, Ibnee."

Rachel walked out of the kitchen nearly forgetting she was wearing an apron.

"Naseem , Naseem , slow down. Don't you want me to change?" She asked looking down at her light blue denim jeans, white Vans and gray Spelman hoodie.

"No, what you are wearing is fine. I'm the one who's overdressed. At least for now."

Rachel blushed tucking her hair behind her ear. Her first time with him the other night was good despite the hiccups. They went down to his white 2019 Range Rover HSE and drove off.

"Where are you taking me? Rachel asked putting on her seatbelt.

"To one of my favorite hotspots." Naseem laced his fingers with hers.

Naseem continued driving down the bluff. When they reached the location, Naseem got out and stripped down to his boxers.

"Are you joining me?" He extended his hand. Rachel followed taking off her shoes and pants but keeping on her underwear and hoodie. They carefully walked around the bluff that shielded their vision looking down on the waters below. There were others surrounding different pockets of water nearby.

"Ready?" Naseem said holding her hand.

"What do you...oh no you don't mean...Ooh, hell no!" She screamed as they dove off a cliff, popping up in the water seconds later. Naseem laughed and Rachel splashed him while removing her hair from her face. They then swam towards a cave.

"Wow," Rachel said stepping onto a cool stone once they were at the entrance. There was a large smooth rock in the front. Rachel walked pass and caressed it.

"Come, my lady."

Rachel saw depictions of an ancient language and drawings as they continued walking. It became cooler and darker inside, the deeper they went in. Rachel shivered as her wet hoodie clung to her.

"Hold on. We're almost there."

Soon enough, Rachel saw a green and purple light which caused her to gasp. It was a purple underwater cave covered by what looked to be glowing green stalagmites. As Rachel looked closer, she saw it was decorated with translucent purple stones. The stones reflected off the sunlight from the tiny holes in the cave above.

"Wow."

Rachel removed her hoodie and stepped into the

water. The cold she felt was long forgotten. "This is incredible. We must come back and take pictures." Rachel moved around the water. "And these stalagmites, how do they glow?" Rachel touched one, instead of it not moving, it wiggled in her hand.

"Those are not stalagmites, look closely, they're moving.'

"Oh my goodness." Rachel yanked her hand away. "Eww, I'm a chemist not a biologist." "Are these eels or snakes?"

Naseem laughed. "Glow worms to be exact. They're harmless."

Naseem continued laughing while Rachel splashed the water and continued moving around. "I feel this is a very special place. I'm glad you brought me here."

"Come to me, habibtee."

Naseem was laid back against a rock. They cuddled enjoying each other's presence. Rachel closed her eyes as she felt the cave's calmness.

"Are you nervous about us?" Naseem asked.

"No to be honest, the wedding is the easiest part. I'm enjoying the preparations with Atiya. How do you feel about it?"

"Al hamdulilah, I will finally be able to call you my wife. But it isn't happening fast enough if you ask me."

"It will be nice to finally sleep in your bed, and wake up next to you."

"And start a family." He said kissing her.

"About that. How do you feel about adopting Rayan? I know that it sounds a bit weird. Of coarse, he will not have rights to the throne but I think it will set a good example."

"I agree but in our society, we don't adopt. However, we'll take them in. Honestly, I have really grown to respect the little guy. He's smart. I got word this morning he's excelling already in school." "But I know you know that. I see you going over his homework with him every night. You must love him dearly."

"I do Naseem I really do. I know I kind of fell into this motherhood thing so soon. I want to make sure he never suffers again, and actually has a chance in life."

"Well, it's settled then. We will officially take him in. We can hold a private ceremony whenever you desire."

"Ok."

They sat in silence once again. Naseem was massaging Rachel's thighs as she sat on his lap facing opposite. She kept her eyes closed as Naseem shifted but calm turned to desire when she felt his dick pressing up on her ass. She tried ignoring it, but Naseem began moving his hands up and down. Rachel pretended not to notice as his hands began traveling northward. Her love language was the right touch, and anytime Naseem caressed her, it was surely her weakness. He unhooked her bra, pushed it out of the way and began plucking her nipples.

"Naseem." Rachel moaned as he ignored and continued to plucking. Naseem then fondled her left breast as his right hand slipped downwards. He started playing with her clit causing Rachel to moan as she moven around on his lap. "Naseeeem."

The bad boy got her juices flowing; easily slipping inside her wet pussy; in and out of her as she rocked back and forth. He whispered her name every few seconds and then added two instead of one. Stroking in and out, Naseem continued plucking her nipple. His dick was hard as rock.

"Give me m--oooooore." Rachel begged opening her legs wider so that he could poke deeper. Naseem complied thrusting deeper.

"Oooooouuuu." Rachel arched back on his neck french-kissing him. With each stroke, she moved back and forth causing his dick to grow harder. Naseem wanted to make her cum in this state, but he had had enough.

He lifted her up and Rachel stared glazed in desire. His dick busted through the opening of his boxers. He gestured for her to turn around. Rachel braced on both sides of his thighs as she slowly lowered herself onto his dick. She thought that they would start off slow, but Naseem had other plans. He lifted her in position and pushed his dick in.

"Ohhhh!," Rachel let out. The feeling of her wet walls cradling him tightly was almost too much to bear.

"You like it?" Naseem said as he clutching her hair beginning ready to beat that pussy up.

"Yes, aaaah, yes, Oh daddy, Oh!."

"Yes, who?" He slapped her ass as she went up and down.

"You, daddy." Naseem fucked her faster. He liked when Rachel acted submissive and called him daddy, but homegirl was never one to play submissive for too long. Rachel placed her hands on the cool rocks behind him. Bracing herself, she lifted up and began slamming herself down on his dick.

"Shit." Naseem groaned as he held on.

"Now, do you like that?"

"Oh! Yes."

"Yes, who?" She asked pulling on his bottom lip.

"Yes, my queen." Naseem smacked her on the ass again and Rachel continued riding with a vengeance. He sucked on her breasts, going from left to right which drove Rachel wild.

"Oh, oh, oh.."

"Mmmm, I can feel that pussy getting close to explode." Naseem said biting her nipples.

"Fuck, Shit, Fuck, Naseem, don't stop, don't stop,

don't stop, ooooooooooooh." Rachel orgasmed and scratched Naseem's back in the process.

Naseem quickly took the doggystyle position; pushing deep inside, one hand on her hip and the other on her shoulder. Rachel arched back as he fucked her hard. The stroke echoed a resounding smack throughout the cave. Rachel 's pussy was dripping down her thighs. She reached for Naseem's arm and held his hip as his dick started tensing. "Fuck me, fuck me, ooooooo!." Rachel let off another orgasm.

Naseem continued fucking until he came.

"Fuuuuccccccck." He grabbed both sides of her ass, letting loose while continue to ram. Moments later, Naseem collapsed beside her. Rachel smiled cuddling up next to him.

"That was...I don't even know what to say," said Rachel breathing heavily.

"Incredible, amazing, the best. I'm at lost for words."

"Ok, Mr. Conceited. Why do I feel as if you're only going to become more possessive after I give you some?"

"Because you already know me so well."

They laughed and kissed for a while before getting up.

"Come on, let's swim this off. Dinner should be ready soon."

CHAPTER FIFTEEN

*R*achel and Naseem held hands as the gates opened to the palace. Rachel was then escorted to her room where Rafiq waited outside for her to change. She put on a pink chiffon dress which complimented Naseem's blue suit nicely. They then walked arm and arm to the dining room and arrived just as Atiyah was placing the last dish on the table. Sitting were Atiyah, Fadi, Haithum and his wife, Maryam who was pregnant. Where Rayan sat, were two boys looking devilish who Rachel assumed were Haithum and Linah's two sons, Nasir and Numair. They were around Rayan's age.

"Boys." Maryam said softly and they all stopped playing.

"Let's eat."

Naseem sat at the head and Rachel on his right as everyone began passing dishes.

"Omi, this looks delicious. You'll have to tell me what all of this is." Rachel said filling her plate. "That is baba ghanoush, the other is fattoush and these are waraqa-eenab."

At dinner, the family chatted and enjoyed their meal. The boys then went outside to play. Haithum kept winking at Naseem as Rachel told those present about her plans for the orphans and animals. Naseem elbowed Haithum when his wife, Maryam told everyone they were expecting a third child; a baby girl.

The family atmosphere was soothing until Naseem's aunt, Jamelia and cousin Kaseem arrived. Kaseem shook hands with the men as Jamelia sat next to the ladies; looking Rachel up and down. "And you are?"

"This is Naseem's fiancé, Rachel." Atiyah said grasping Rachel's shoulder. "Isn't she beautiful? I can't wait until she and my son marry and give me some Abnaa."

That statement caused Rachel to blush.

"And when will you be getting married?"

"They'll be married by Naseem's 25th birthday and I'm sure they will quickly get started on making our next heirs." Atiyah always made her sister feel like her daughter.

"Ok, I see," said Jamelia. "Well, Kaseem and I must be on our way. Yallah." She waved toward her son.

"I'll see you out, Uktee." Atiya said getting up.

When they left, Rachel asked Maryam,"What's with those two?"

"Atiyah and Jamelia have a bad sister relationship. They've competed with each other since they were younger. If you and Naseem do not get married, the throne will then go to her son, Kaseem which is exactly what Jamelia wants. He is nice young man but his mother on the other hand is a—"

"Don't say it."

"I'm serious. That woman thinks her son is the best man in Omash."

"Sounds like her prediction will be wrong."

"All of this got me tired." Maryam said wadding over to her husband.

Naseem and Rachel walked them to the door as Hibba took Rayan to take a bath before bed.

"You did really well today," said Naseem embracing Rachel.

"Yeah, standing like a deer caught in headlights with your Aunt and trying not to stare at you and think about what happened earlier."

"That's not what I saw."

"What did you see?" Rachel said fiddling with his collar.

"I saw you getting along great with my sister-andlaw, letting my mom show off as she loves to do, being attentive and caring to Rayan. Also, you showed my family what an amazing queen you will be."

"You saw all that?" Rachel kissed him nonstop.

"And so much more." Naseem pinched her butt.

"Let's put Rayan to bed before we..."

"Go to bed?"

"Yes, let's--" Naseem said as he chased Rachel down the hall.

———

The next morning, Rachel remembered to reply to her mother's message.

Mom,

I am glad everyone is doing okay. There is so much I want to tell you but I honestly don't know where to begin. I told you I met someone. Mom, I'll cut to the chase. I'm in love in a way I've never been before. The guy makes me feel treasured, protected and above all else like a lady. He's very powerful but does not to wield his power over me. He's smart, wise and although he can have the weight of the world on his shoulders, you would never know. He reminds me of dad. I want to be with him forever and we plan on marrying before the end of the year. I'd love for you to come visit this beautiful country. I promise to reach out to you soon. Love you mom.

— FOREVER & ALWAYS. LOVE,

RACHEL

Rachel hit send and closed her laptop. She and Atiya had a day full of wedding preparations ahead. She wanted to ask Naseem if he could arrange for her family to be there knowing it would be interesting to see how her brothers would react. The thought made her chuckle.

Rachel went into the lounge area with Atiya. The wedding planner and Aunt Jamelia were already there.

"Sabahul Kaiyr, Auntie."

"Sabahul Noor, young child...what's your name again? Keisha? Monique? Yolanda?"

"It's Rachel—" Rachel was about to snap but was interrupted by her mother-in-law.

"This woman will be queen soon, so it won't be hard to forget."

"Really?"

"So—" Rachel said changing subjects. "Before we get back into the preparations, I want to plan a party for Naseem's 25th birthday. I don't want our wedding to overshadow his day."

"What did you have in mind?" asked Atiya.

"Something small. No more than 50 people."

"That's impossible." Atiya and Jamelia said at once. They then stared at each other; agreeing on something for once.

"There's no way with a list of less than three hundred. We would offend the dignitaries."

"Hmm, ok. I've got it. Let's have an open screen movie viewing. I believe the Lion King would be great since the remake is coming out. My girl Beyonce got a part in it. You know?"

Atiya and Jamelia shrugged not knowing what Rachel was talking about.

"Anyway, your son told me he likes animation movies. I think he'd get a kick out of it if the boys dressed up as some cartoon characters."

"As you wish, my lady but--" said Atiyah while Jamelia wasn't impressed.

"So let's decorate the North Ballroom with action movie posters. We should have popcorn, all types of candy especially cotton, nachos, ice cream, Skittles, Twizzlers, hot dogs, soft drinks and some of y'all favorite snacks. You got that?" said Rachel to the wedding planner who was jotting down what she could.

"Sorry, Sayyida. I'm not familiar with these things," replied the wedding planner whose job clearly wasn't taking inventory.

"Don't worry about it. I'll pull them up on Amazon, email you and you can order them."

"Ok, my lady."

"What about a photo booth? I know you, young people like those." Atiyah said laughing while shaking her head.

"Yes, mom. That's a good idea. The one with the funny props."

"Enough, it's settled then. A surprise movie birthday for my nephew. Now, let's get back to the wedding preparations. What day is it?" asked Jamelia.

"Oh Jamelia, we can't let all of the secrets out. You'll have to wait for the invitation."

Cutting the small talk, the wedding planner interrupted. "What colors would you like, Sayyida Rachel?"

"Purple and Gold, baby! The colors of the Los Angeles Lakers."

"What a good choice!" Atiyah said patting Rachel not knowing who Rachel was talking about again.

"I know we have to have the wedding at the Grand Hall and it's typically a showcase. However, it is important for Naseem and I to mix traditional and my customs."

"Ok."

"Naseem and I do not want to be separated. We'll keep the tradition of being separated before the wedding but we want to be together during it. That's my only request."

"Plating, flowers, cake?" The wedding planner interjected again.

"Rose gold plating and accents. Naseem and I don't have a preference for flowers, crystals or candelabras. But the cake should be yellow with buttercup icing. Everything else we'll leave up to you, Omi and Auntie."

"Mumtaz, now let's go over the wedding invitations. I think this background would go nicely, don't you think?" asked the wedding planner.

"Yes, it's perfect."

Hours later, Rachel watched as Rayan played in the courtyard. Her thoughts drifted to her future husband. "Sayyida Rachel, Sayyida Rachel!!" Maha yelled as she ran into the courtyard.

"Nam, what is it?"

"The women of the tribes have summoned for you. They can't come to an agreement about the orphans and seek your consul right away."

"Have Rafiq bring the car around."

"Rayan!" Rachel yelled. "Would you like to come with me or are you staying here with Maha?"

"I want to go with you, my queen."

"Ok, my protector."

CHAPTER SIXTEEN

*W*hen Rachel arrived, she saw more women and children than before. As she walked deeper into the encampment, the murmurs of *"It's the queen, it's the queen"* followed. The women bowed as she came upon a large gathering. Rafiq and Hibba followed close behind with a group of guards while Rayan held Rachel's hand. She approached an older woman who appeared to be in charge. "How can I help?" Hibba began interpreting.

"Sayyida, more fighting has lead to a larger number of displaced children. Our families are not able to feed everyone. We've heard stories of how you took that boy there and how you care deeply for the young. We sought this counsel to find out what to do."

"I see."

"For those that are old enough to work, let's find out from the villages who are willing to act as host families. And for those that are too young, I will set up safe havens in the unused buildings here for now and contact establishments in the capital to ensure that you receive supplies. Who would like to volunteer to look after a group of five children a piece before the supplies come?"

"Ana! My queen," rang out throughout the women.

"I had plans to begin setting up safe zones in a few months but there is no better time to start than now. We'll work together to make sure these children are taken care of and not forgotten. Remember, we are not separate tribes and villages, we're one community. I may be your future queen, but I am just like you and I will work as hard. I'll come as often as needed until everything is settled. I'll need for you all to begin making preparations tonight. Please gather all of the children at the school and I'll contact the housing minister at once." Rachel stated.

"Thank you, my queen." The women said smiling and bowing.

"Laa Shukran Wajib."

Back at the car, Hibba and Rafiq sat inside making calls. Within two hours, the food, bedding, and rein-forcements were on its way along with a few troops. As Rachel separated the women into groups and began organizing what should be done and where the children should go, she couldn't shake the feeling of Omash people constantly watching her. The trucks began arriving and Rachel assisted.

Later that evening, all of the encampment's orphans were housed and happily running around inside the school.

"How were you able to get them so many toys?" Hibba asked.

"I just told Rafiq to tell them."

"Yallah, I'm tired. Let's go."

"Ok, my queen."

"Hey, I'll see you tomorrow. Masalama." Rachel said to the women as she departed with her entourage.

The sun had gone down hours ago and Rachel knew she should have been home by now.

Rachel arrived back home holding a sleeping Rayan. Before the guards opened the gates, Bashir, Naseem's personal butler, was there with one angry Naseem.

"Rafiq, take Rayan to his bedroom now. Everyone else, leave us! Yallah!" Naseem walked into the study hall and Rachel followed.

"I take it you're upset with me." Rachel said removing her jacket.

"How dare you disobey me!?!"

"Naseem, what do you mean?" Rachel said rubbing his chest trying to diffuse the situation.

"No, you're not going to distract me. You directly disobeyed my orders. I told you never to go to that region without me."

"Naseem, I went with the guards and Rafiq. Isn't he one of your most trusted, second only to Hamid who guards you."

"Yes, but—" Naseem began but Rachel cut him off.

"I also didn't go secretly." Rachel began removing her scarf.

"Everyone knew where I had gone and I left a message telling you where and why."

"Yes, but—"

"You're scared. I know you aren't used to a woman like me."

"I don't want to lose you."

"I know, baby. I don't want to lose you either. I love you, Naseem." Rachel said kissing him.

"You cannot continue to be so reckless. We aren't married yet and it is not safe for you to travel without protection or a mahram." Naseem said between kisses.

"Who would dare defy you? The mighty sultan. No one wants to face your wrath," declared Rachel pulling his tie.

"Some will still try."

"And we will conquer them together. I'm sorry. If

you want me to take more guards I will. There were plenty of women and I was never alone."

"I know those people aren't fighting anymore but there are still rumblings. You must have at least fifty guards with you until we have total peace."

"Ok. I will do as you ask."

"By the way, how'd it go?"

"It went well. I didn't plan on starting yet but I'm actually glad things happened this way. I was able to get most of the resources we need sent but I will need your help however. It would be great if I could meet with someone in the ministry of finance to discuss the best way to protect them." Rachel said licking her lip as her mind drifted.

"Already taken care of. Here's the number of the man, you will be speaking with. His name is Humaid. When you told me of your idea, I had him research it. He can assist you with everything you need and if you need more money, just ask."

Naseem came up behind her and holding her by the waist.

"How did I get so lucky?" Rachel turned around and looking Naseem in the eyes.

"I ask myself the same thing every day." Naseem said kissing her.

"Let's go watch a movie alone."

"No chick flicks." Naseem held her hand as they walked toward the home theatre. "

"You can pick the movie. It's your turn anyway," said Rachel sticking her tongue out.

Two hours later, the movie ended. "That was amazing! The way the big green guy smashed those little ones and the man with shield threw it like a boomerang, and the man with the hammer."

"Do you even know the name of movie, Naseem?"

"The Fantastic Four?"

"Please, don't. It was the Avengers: Endgame. You weren't even paying attention."

"I was joking. I knew that."

Rachel began fanning herself. "Hey, let's go to bed, we have a long week ahead of us."

And that they did. The week was full of Rachel in the villages working with the community setting up the safe zones for the orphans and stray animals. Her days were so long that there were nights she didn't even see Naseem. But, they left notes for each other. Between expanding business into more regions and ensuring the newly established community continued to work together peacefully, Naseem had his hands full.

As the days got closer and closer to Naseem's birthday and their wedding date, things got busier.

CHAPTER SEVENTEEN

*T*wo weeks later, Rachel woke up alone after a long nap. She stretched like a cat before calling Maha.

"I can't believe we are 2 ½ weeks away from the wedding." Maha said excitedly.

"I know, all of the wedding invitations have been sent and we will be married the night before Naseem's birthday."

"Are you nervous?" Maha asked as she brushed Rachel 's hair. Rachel turned around, licked her lips and played with the ends as she replied,"I've never been a queen before and never expected this."

"I know Atiyah will be here to help, but I don't want to mess this up. There are so many people." Rachel mentioned.

"Let your love of the people and your compassion guide you. You are human, you aren't perfect."

"I know. You're right. Is everything set for the party tonight?" Rachel asked switching topics.

"Everything is ready, my lady. Everyone will be here in the next hour or so and Naseem should be arriving thirty minutes after that," said Maha.

Rachel decided to speed up Naseem's party so it was a surprise and wouldn't overshadow their wedding.

"Tayyib," said Rachel walking over to her closet. She pulled out a Lara Croft costume.

"I'm going to get ready. Meet me in the ballroom in thirty minutes. I want to do a final walk through and make sure everything is set."

"Ajal, Sayyida. "

"No, no, no, the posters need to be raised higher, those are way too low to the ground," said Rachel. The girl from Atlanta was decked out in her Lara Croft costume. Rafiq manned the door and was wearing a black suit looking sharper than ever. When Rachel joked if he and his brother were dressed as the Men in Black, he said he did not get her. Maha wore a Kill Bill outfit and Hibba resembled Chung Li from Street Fighter. Atiya and the rest of the family arrived wearing different superhero outfits. Rayan ran around the theater dressed as Woody from Toy Story with Nasir and Numair who were dressed as Iron Man and

Batman. Out of all the costume's, Fadi's was the most interesting. He dressed as Rambo.

Rachel hurried everyone inside the movie theater. Presents on one side while the family was on the other.

"He's here!" Bashir said, coming into the room.

"Perfect. Everyone crouch down. Bashir, go get the birthday boy."

Rachel grabbed Rayan and crouched in the corner. Naseem followed Bashir to the theatre after being told that his future wife was waiting for him. He hoped Rachel wasn't going to watch another set of chick flicks. She made him watch all of the Bridget Jones movies. Naseem shook his head as they approached. After the day he had, he was only waiting for Rachel's legs to be spread wide in front of the big screen.

As soon as they arrived, everyone immediately jumped out and yelled "Surprise". Rachel ran to Naseem and kissed him. Naseem was shocked.

"Happy birthday, baby." Rachel said kissing him again.

"You did this for me." Naseem said ruffling Rayan's head.

His mother and sister came over to hug him and then he shook hands and hugged everyone else.

"Why are you not dressed like us?" Rayan asked.

"I didn't get the memo." Naseem said chuckling.

Rachel went to the corner over and brought

Naseem his costume. "Hurry and get dressed, so we can start the movie. You don't want to miss your party."

Naseem came back 10 minutes later dressed as his favorite action hero, Jean Claude Van Damme. Everyone settled in their seats and soon the opening credits for "Bloodsport" were running across the screen.

"How did you come up with all of this?" Naseem laced his hands with Rachel's.

"I just wanted your birthday to be special. I felt like the wedding would overshadow it and while we are all busy planning, your birthday is still very special."

"I love you."

"I love you, too."

The opening scene started, snapping them out of their reverie. Naseem's older brother, Haithum was falling asleep during the movie, so Rachel and Maryam woke him up by dumping popcorn on him. After the movie ended, Naseem opened his gifts, thanked his guests and hurriedly rushed everyone out of the house.

"He could only be rushing everyone out for one reason," thought Rachel.

After putting Rayan to bed, Naseem walked

Rachel to her bedroom. She opened the door and was surprised when his hands stopped her at the door knob. "What...are you not coming in?"

"No, I have some work to do tonight...but I wanted to thank you for everything. This really meant a lot to me."

"No problem." Rachel bent kissing his palm. Naseem kissed hers back and said,"Get some rest."

"Don't work too hard, boo."

Two days went by slowly and Rachel felt as if Naseem was avoiding her. She had barely seen him and when she did, he was very busy. She was surprised when he picked her up from work that night with Rayan. Naseem was dressed nicely and Rayan was also; wearing a cream colored suit with a lavender shirt.

"Sayyida Rachel!" Rayan said when he had come to get Rachel. "The Sultan is taking us to dinner. Hurry!" Rayan tugged her arm. Rachel went downstairs where Naseem was waiting.

"Where are we going?"

"You'll see, honey."Rachel got in seeing that her guards were nowhere to be seen, which was odd.

They drove in silence as Rachel 's anticipation heightened. Thirty minutes later, they arrived at the Coast of Pearls. There was a candlelight path which made its way to a stone gazebo. A stone platform was topped with lighter stone pillars and arches on each side. On the platform itself, there were sheer white curtains draping revealing a welcoming entrance. The seating area was filled with candles of all sorts which surrounded an ornate table covered in gladiolus and dahlia flowers. On the table were rose-gold dishes filled with Briyani, lamb, goat, fried chicken, different kinds of rice, pieces of bread, and soups. Rachel sat after Naseem pulled out her chair. Rachel dished out servings and then began eating, moaning, ."Mmm, this is delicious."

They enjoyed their meal while chatting about the latest events.

"Thank you for this amazing meal with my two favorite boys. Now, what's the special occasion?"

"Well, I'm glad you asked. Rayan, are you ready to show Rachel?" The boy nodded and came around the table to stand in the middle of where Rachel and Naseem were seated.

"Close your eye, Sayyida Rachel and no peeking."

Rachel turned and chuckled.

"Ok, you can open them."

When Rachel opened her eyes, she saw a man she had never seen before holding a book and Naseem was nowhere to be found. As Rachel stood up and looked, she asked,"Where's Naseem?"Rayan tugged on her to follow him. They walked around the gazebo and found another candlelight path. On his knees, in the middle of a candle and lilac circle was Naseem .

As Rachel approached, Rayan ran over to Naseem and kneeled, too. Together they hummed,"*Sayyida Rachel, zawajana...*" "*Layla, min fadlik.*" Then, Rayan sang other words in a melodic tone. Rachel covered her mouth as her tears began falling. She extended her hand as Naseem slipped a rose gold ring on her ring finger.

"Humayr has agreed to officiate our wedding and the adoption ceremony."

"But what about the family?"

"This wedding will just be for the three of us. We will still have our big one for the world to see." Pulling her out of sight of the others, Naseem explained that it's tradition for the royal family to wed in secret before the public one. The custom has been passed down from generation to generation out of necessity. There have been so many attempts to seize the throne, so it was imperative that once a match is made, that the marriage must happen this way."

"And...and after my surprise birthday, I decided why wait. The next time I lay with you, I want to be your husband."

"Ok. I think I understand," said Rachel biting her nails confused and nervous.

"As for what you will wear, I've brought a few wedding dresses. Pick one and get changed over there," Naseem said pointing to a guest lounge area.

Twenty minutes later, Rachel slowly walked up the beach to join Rayan and Naseem, now both dressed in white Khandooras with gold cufflinks and head attire. Rachel wore a white strapless dress. The bodice of the gown was decorated in a design of Naseem's family crest. It was molded to Rachel's curves and transitioned in a line down her middle giving way to a flare at the bottom that revealed its flowery designs. Rachel's veil formed a train behind her as she walked.

"You look so beautiful," said Rayan hugging Rachel 's leg.

"Thank you, my boy." Rachel began sniffling.

Humayr began the adoption ceremony by giving a lovely story about family and how blood is not the only thing that binds us. When Humayr finished, Rayan pulled out a piece of paper and read:

"Sultan and Sultana, when you found me that day, I was homeless and had nowhere to go. Sultana Rachel saw something in me and decided to take me in. I am forever grateful. I vow to always be your protector, to always make you proud. I love you, Sultana."

He gave Rachel a kiss that she bent down to receive.

"...And Sultan Naseem. I promise to be just like you when I grow up, to always protect your queen, to make good decisions and be brave. May Allah protect you."

The boy was given his papers showing legal guardianship under Rachel and Naseem and everyone present yelled *Allahu Akbar, Allahu Akbar.*

"This concludes the adoption ceremony and now for the marriage.

"Who has come to bear witness to this union?" Rafiq and Hamid stepped forward.

"Al hamdulilah, marriage is a sacred commitment made by two individuals. It is the binding of love, it is a partnership awarded by the one above all. We tie the hands to symbolize the sanctity of this union." Himayar stated as he pulled out several ribbons. "The yellow ribbon symbolizes attraction, balance and harmony." He stated as he tied a love knot. "The purple ribbon symbolizes health, strength, healing and power...and finally the green ribbon symbolizes fertility, beauty, prosperity, luck and love." "Let these knots be a representation of the bond you make this evening." "Now, do you, Rachel Johnson take thee Sultan Naseem Naseem Al Said Hamaad born of Atiya and Shammar Al Said Hamaad of the Al Said Hamaad dynasty, to have and to hold, in sickness and in health, for richer or for poor, til your return to Allah."

"I do." She responded, squeezing Naseem's hands and looking him in the eyes.

"Do you Sultan of Omash, Protector of this land, Chosen Son of the Al Said Hamaad Dynasty born Naseem Naseem Al Said Hamaad take thee Rachel Johnson, born to Charles and Charlotte Johnson of Atlanta, Georgia, to have and hold, in sickness and in health, for richer or for poorer, til your return to Allah?"

"I do." Naseem said.

"By the power vested in me, I now pronounce you husband and wife; sultan and sultana."

Naseem pulled Rachel in to a heart-stopping kiss. Rachel saw fireworks in the air, shocked that her and Naseem were officially married.

CHAPTER EIGHTEEN

The ceremony concluded and Rafiq drove them home. Rayan fell asleep on the way and when they arrived home, Hamid carried the boy to bed. Naseem told Rachel he would sneak in her room for the next few days before the wedding but tonight he would spend the night with her.

"I believe you're supposed to carry me across the threshold." Rachel stated. She giggled when Naseem picked her up and did just that.

"Let's take a bath first." Rachel turned her back so Naseem could unzip her dress. She began running the water and eased into the warmness of the tub and sighed when it touched her melanin skin. The bathroom reminded her of a sauna and the tub was big enough to fit four. Naseem slipped in soon after. Rachel blew bubbles at him and played with his chest hairs while they kissed.

"We're married. I don't believe this? Wow!"

"Yes, we are, my queen." Naseem said as he kissed her foot and began up her thighs. "Open your legs." Rachel raised her eyebrows but obliged. Naseem began stroking the insides of her thighs. He pulled her closer so that her legs were propped over his and began kissing her on the neck.

"Mmm," Rachel moaned as Naseem licked and bit her. "Baby." Rachel's body began to tingle. The bubbles along with the hairs on Naseem's arms were making her nipples achy and tender. She relaxed as he played with them. "Oooooo!" Rachel moaned as he drowned her sound with kisses. Naseem began licking from her mouth...down her neck...to her beautiful dark nipples. Naseem sucked the left one as he fondled the right.

"Oh shit!" Rachel moaned.

All she wanted was to fuck her husband. Rachel moved her hand down to her pussy and began finger-fucking herself. Naseem's dick got harder as he watched his wife insert in and out. He then came over and licked Rachel 's fingers.

"Mommy's pussy is good ain't it." Rachel took a long lick of her fingers.

"Now lick them again."

Rachel put her fingers into her mouth and sucked every ounce of juice there was. She then reached for Naseem's dick, watching his reaction.

"Go wait in the bedroom, bad girl. Yallah!" He smacked Rachel's ass which turned her on even more.

When Naseem came in, he found Rachel laying sideways, with her head hanging off the mattress.

"Naseem." She began stroking his dick as he was getting into position. Rachel changed positions.

"Because this is our first time as husband and wife, I have a special request."

"Go on." Naseem asked rubbing his cock on her pussy and getting ready to push it in. Rachel sucked her lips nervously and didn't like being so vulgar.

"Speak."

"I want you to stand in front of me and put your dick in my mouth. Push it in deeply. I will choke… while you eat and finger my pussy at the same time."

"And?" Nassem said simply as he bit her nipples and continued to rub his cock against her pussy.

"Just fuck the shit out of me, boy!"

Naseem stood in front of Rachel and slowly began inserting inch after inch of his dick into her watery mouth. Rachel was in heaven and had fantasized for weeks about sucking Naseem's dick like this. Naseem pushed slowly inch by inch. Every time he fully pushed inside, Rachel moaned in ecstasy and her pussy got wetter in response. When he continued to stay go deep in her throat, she stroked and clutched his balls. Naseem groaned as he looked at his wife splayed below. It turned him on to know that his wife was so naughty. Rachel tits jiggled with each stroke deeper and deeper into her throat; the saliva was wetting everything. Naseem moved his hand down and clutched her nipples on the way to her pussy. He started off playing slowly on her clit. Rachel moaned as Naseem started making it do smacking noises. She gagged on his cock harder as Naseem played more.

"Fuck." Naseem switched positions to eat Rachel out. Her wetness was dripping down his goatee. He eased one finger, then two in as he continued to work on her clit with his tongue. Rachel groaned as she continued sucking deeper, watering Naseem's balls. She backed away and turned to the side to circle her tongue around his tip before putting it back in. Naseem bought a dildo; removing his fingers and replaced them with it. Letting it fully insert, Naseem slowly moved it in and out.

"Fuck"

They were both getting closer and closer to climaxing.

"Baaaaaabbbbbbyyyy." Rachel moaned as she felt her pussy clench around the dildo. "Mmmmmm, fuck baby, don't stop." Rachel moaned as she kept sucking almost choking from so much saliva.

"Fuck baby." She moaned,"I mean it..." She panted. "I don't want...mmmm baby...I don't want my first orgasm as your wife to be...mmm...to be without your cock in me."

Naseem was seconds away from cumming down her throat. Rachel sighed when he removed his dick from her mouth. He flipped her over and pulled her to the edge of the bed so that she was now standing but laying over the bed. Rachel moaned as Naseem teased her with the dildo.

"Pleeeaaassse, baby." Rachel moaned.

"Please what?" Naseem said spanking her ass cheek.

"Please fuck me now, daddy. I need your dick in me."

Rachel bent over. Naseem pushed an inch of his dick into her and then quickly withdrew. He continued this going deeper and deeper each time. They moaned when he was fully inside. Naseem grabbed her curly hair and began pumping in and out. Shallow thrust, shallow thrust then deep. Shallow thrust, shallow thrust, then deep. With each thrust, Naseem's pelvis hit the right motion.

"Fuck" he groaned as her pussy began to clutch and squeeze his cock. Naseem could feel Rachel about to cum and he wasn't far behind. Grabbing her hair in one hand and her titty in the other, he deeply pounded as Rachel yelled in pain and pleasure.

"Fuck baby, aaaaaaaaah,aaaaaaahhhhh." Rachel moaned as she began cumming.

"Fuck, oh, oh, oh shit!" Naseem grunted as he

came inside her right at the same time. He was shaking like a mad man and Rachel held his hips in her pussy tightly to take all of his cum.

She laid back and moaned as Naseem got up and went to the bathroom. He came back and she laid on his chest.

"I cannot...(kiss) believe...(kiss) we...(kiss) just did that."

"Give me a few minutes and we're going to start again...and again."

———

And they did, two more times before the night was over.

The next morning Naseem slipped away unnoticed by everyone in the house; making sure to leave a smile on his wife's face before he left.

CHAPTER NINETEEN

*T*wo days later, Rachel was at work on the phone.

"Yes, honey...Rayan and I will see you later...yes (giggle)...oooou and what else is my husband going to do after dinner...mmmm...with your hands or your mouth...stop it, Naseem. I'm getting off the phone with you. Yes, I am, (giggle), I love you too. Bye."

Rachel ended the call.

"Sultana Rachel!" Her secretary said knocking on her door.

"Yes, Abeer?"

"Your car's waiting downstairs."

Rachel grabbed her purse and headed towards the door.

"I'm going to check on the lab and then I'll be right down. Please, let Rafiq know."

"Ajaal." Melanie replied while she began dialing the line.

Rachel went into lab and hummed as she checked the instruments. "Well, that doesn't look good." She put her purse down in front of the GC-MS and raised her eyebrows as she began troubleshooting the instrument. She was so deep into concentration she didn't notice the maintenance man coming until he was a foot away.

"Marhaban," greeted the man.

"Marhaban beak." Rachel turned around startled.

When did a white man start working here?

"I see you've learned a bit of Arabic while you've been here."

"Yes, sir, but how can I help you?"

"You have a very handsome little boy."

"Thank you. Again, how can I help you?"

"If you want him to stay that way, I advise you to come with me."

"What?!?"

Rachel struggled fighting off the man but before she knew it, the man had a bag over her face. She inhaled ether and she fastly became unconscious. The man lifted her up and put her in a trash bin. He then headed to the back freight elevator going to the rear delivery entrance. Once he landed, he loaded the bin onto a truck.

Fifteen minutes later, Rafiq came off the elevator to Rachel's floor. "Shufta, Sultana Rachel ?" He looked worried as he kept looking at his watch. It was not like Rachel to be late.

"She must still be in the lab," Abeer replied shrugging.

Rafiq went down to the lab and called out,"Sultana, Sultana." He looked around but did not find her. He went back upstairs to Abeer and said,"Pull up the cameras to the entrances and elevators. Yallah! Yallah!"

"Ajaal, Rafiq!"

They watched a white man come inside the back of the building from the delivery area. A truck waited and then pulled off ten minutes later with the man and a bin.

"Lock down the building. Alert security. The Americans." Rafiq shouted as he raced down the stairs. When he and his entourage made it to the back entrance, Rachel was long gone. Rafiq made the one phone call he never wanted to.

When the line picked up, he said,"Sultan...Rachel's gone. The Americans got her."

CPSIA information can be obtained
at www.ICGtesting.com
Printed in the USA
LVHW090326021019
632927LV00001BA/90/P